A MODERN WAY TO DIE

A MODERN

WAY TO DIE

SMALL STORIES
&
MICROTALES

DIE

by
PETER WORTSMAN

Fromm International Publishing Corporation
NEW YORK

Library of Congress Cataloging-in-Publication Data
Wortsman, Peter.
A modern way to die : small stories and microtales / by Peter
Wortsman.—1st ed.
p.   cm.
ISBN 0-88064-133-9 (alk. paper) : $17.95
I. Title.
PS3573.O77M63   1991
813'.54—dc20   91-17416

To my father's memory

Nichts dauert ewig,
Der schänste Jud wird schäbig.

Viennese proverb

die . . . I. Of man and sentient
beings . . . I.a. *intr.* To lose life,
cease to live, suffer death; to expire . . . 7.d. To experience a sexual
orgasm. (Most common as a poetical
metaphor in the late 16th and 17th
cent.)

Oxford English Dictionary

Acknowledgments

Of these texts, eight first appeared in 2 PLUS 2: A *Collection of International Writing*: "I Stand Possessionless at the Gate of the Living," "It's Hard to Be a Fish," "Carolina Street," "The Gate," "The Milkman Isn't Coming Anymore," "Photograph of a Kiss," "The Two Collectors," and "The House of Phantasy" (later published in German translation in *Schreibheft*). "A Modern Way to Die" was first published in *Semiotext(e)*. "Wet Pain" and "Sid and Darling" were first published in *Between* C & D. "The Eye of the Beholder" was first published in German translation in *manuskripte*. "Exquisite Scream, According to X," "Stop Playing!," and "It" were first published in *Blue Light Red Light*. "The Human Butterfly" first appeared in *Dreamworks*. "Cornell Listening to a Box of Rice Krispies" and "Are There Any Catfish in the Thames?" were first published in *Paragraph*. The author wishes to thank the editors of those publications and the board of directors of The Beard's Fund for their support in the form of a short story prize.

Contents

I. SMALL STORIES

1. SCREAMS

2. STINGS

II. MICROTALES

1. U<small>RBAN</small> F<small>AUNA</small>

2. B<small>IOCHIPS</small>

3. REFRACTIONS

A Foreword

These small stories appeared in the absence of big things to say, propelled nonetheless (like the rubber-band-icecream-spoon-powered rain puddle boats of our childhood) by the same urge to move, in miniature; to make waves; to push the world aside and skid across its surface; to get from the mundane suffocating *here* to the blessed *over-there*; to strike out, albeit on a limited journey, without map or compass, without destination, guided only by the precarious optimism of the pen.

I. SMALL STORIES

1. SCREAMS

O nce upon a time,

atterns. The
buoyancy: ꞏ
ack to ea
nd fall,
e foot
he spri
f the
ing oꞏ
he m
ear
ized
espe
syꞏ
nd
nd
osi
r r
ꞏs
A

singing with
you feel a pun
hat these elej
ectacles must
ry audiences.
des, the Fre
ve been quit
company wil
te on Septer

•

'ork Danc
the Bessi
né first
oistero
babies
ed,
d
e

A Modern Way
to Die

Once there was a war that no one could see. No bombs exploded. Nobody shrieked. People just dropped dead suddenly. Inexplicably. In the kitchen, in the bedroom, on their weary way home from work. Some said it was heart attack, but too many succumbed to the mysterious affliction for that theory to hold. Others swore it was something in the air: a poison wind from the east, a cosmic inversion.

Though never openly discussed—"cloudy weather" was the favored euphemism—everyone secretly feared being next, and there were those who went so far as to wish it, just to put an end to the unendurable anxiety. But man has an uncanny ability to adapt and make the best of things.

Children started the game, adults followed suit, and soon everyone was at it, picking out prospective victims from the crowd. The talented few, able to point with a deadly accuracy, earned the epithet "golden fingered," and the best of these could command sizable fees to perform in public. Concert halls and stadiums were hired. People flocked to see their favorites.

"Prize fingers," as the papers liked to call them, were invariably shorter than their poster effigies, and despite the blindfold (government regulations), they strode confidently straight to centerstage. Some went in for arabesque antics: twists and turns, and Latin incantations—but the truly great worked with sparse gestures in absolute silence.

A raised palm hushed the crowd. The thumb and three fingers bowed, and the forefinger seemed to grow as it swept out over the sea of anxious eyes, drawn like a compass to the next malignant north. Sometimes a skuffle ensued—the way baseball fans struggle for possession of a homerun or a foul ball, only in reverse: nobody wanted to catch it. But the issue rapidly resolved itself (to the wild delight of spectators) with a sudden squirm and a frenetic hiss, like that of air leaving a balloon. Ushers carted off the corpse, and those seated the closest wiped the sweat off their brows and invariably claimed they'd had their eye on him or her from the start.

Of course there were fakes as there are in every art, individuals lacking in any genuine talent who climb the latest bandwagon for fame and fortune. They hide behind a lot of hocus pocus—and rumor had it that certain charlatans stooped so low as to plant hitmen in the audience to discreetly dispose of predesignated targets on cue.

A great favorite, whose reputation is still the subject of some debate, had black eyes and a finger that drove the women wild. Old maids and teenage girls alike swooned at the sight of him.

"Ladies! . . . Gentlemen!" he whispered, the microphone turned up to capacity, "Look your neighbor in the eye! Can you see? Can you tell? Who is going to be next?" Married women shivered, husbands studied their wives, even young lovers regarded each other with new interest.

"Take me! . . . Take me!" cried the most fervent fans, as the drumroll marked the moment.

What followed at one particular performance has become legend. Eyewitnesses swear that a little boy high up in the bleachers broke the shell of silence. "Hey, Mister!" he cried out, but the master had reached the climax of his act and refused to be disturbed. People tried to still the child. The drumroll swelled, the master's finger swayed. "Mister!" the little boy yelled—heads turned in shock and wonder at the child's audacity—"Mister!" he called, "you're next!"

Stagehands later confirmed how they saw the prize finger tremble and turn white, how one hand clasped the microphone while the other tore off the blindfold, and the crowd's black-eyed darling crumbled to the floor of the stage.

Critics had a heyday, unanimously lambasting the deceased, who had been popular too long, and hailing the boy as a fresh new talent. The incident flickered on in the news till a colorful murder case preempted the spotlight. The boy was said to have made something of a career for himself overseas.

Nowadays, outside of a small circle of diehards, nobody pays much attention to the art anymore. Death has become such a common occurrence that the thrill of guessing has gone out of it. Live combat is back in fashion—war as vivid and spectacular as it once was. People missed the epic sweep and the glorious bang of the bomb.

The House of
Phantasy

"Ich hab' noch einen Koffer in Berlin
Deswegen muss ich nächstens wieder hin . . ."
—Marlene Dietrich

There was a brothel in Berlin during the War that offered a particular pleasure. The house was visited exclu-
sively by officers, ministers of state and high-ranking party
officials who made their way there at night on the sly to
be free for a few hours from the heavy weight of history
and to indulge the sweet torment of their repressed desire.

The gray outer wall of a once magnificent palace faced
the street; its high, black iron gate stood permanently ajar,
forced open no doubt in the long forgotten past and never
again shut.

You crossed the crumbling courtyard, stepping carefully among loose stones and a wilderness of weeds, by-
passed the main entrance, circled 'round to the rear,

climbed three flights up a steep, winding servants' stair-
case, knocked on a plain gray door, seven times lightly—
and then, with the right connections, you were admitted.

The walls of the dark little antechamber in which you
now found yourself were hung with black velvet; and on
the wall directly facing you as you entered, embroidered
in white gothic letters, you read: HIER IST PHANTASIE DER
FUEHRER. (PHANTASY IS THE FUEHRER HERE.)

You removed your hat and coat and handed them
without a word to a dark-haired little chambermaid dressed
in a stern black skirt who quickly and quietly whisked them
away.

Now the moment had come to meet with Frau Alma,
and you shivered with a childish terror—newcomers and
regulars alike: for the old woman knew exactly why you
were there. Frau Alma was by no means a beauty any longer,
yet she carried herself like a woman who knows she can
have anything she wants. She sat motionless in her high-
backed chair and considered each visitor without even turning her head. Her gaunt, white-powdered cheeks brought
to mind a mummy, and when you kissed the long bony
fingers of her outstretched hand it was as though death
had become a woman.

But her sad dark eyes enchanted every man, young or
old. Struck by their gaze, you were at once aroused and
troubled by the odd sensation that these hazelnut orbs
illuminated your soul, perceiving things that even you kept
hidden from yourself. And if you succumbed just once, you
were forevermore addicted—this was no hypnosis, but the
raw force of her woman's nature. Some regulars came twice,
even three times a week; and there were others who for
her sake gave up an honorable career and only still lived
to submit to the urge stirred up by her eyes.

You bowed as to an oriental potentate and brought her treasures the like of which were not easily come by, even in the highest circles of Berlin society: silk, gold jewelry, antique ivory, French cognac, Stradivarius violins, precious stamp collections and other riches recently imported from the eastern regions of the Reich. She nodded her thanks and immediately handed everything over to the little chambermaid. And if Frau Alma was even the least bit pleased, she smiled—not sweetly or seductively, but it was this strange sphinx smile that burst the last chains of your self-control and freed the wild I from its cage. And yet somehow she always made you feel that the gift was not enough, that only out of pity and the goodness of her heart was she letting you enter her house, that you could never even dream of what Frau Alma really wanted.

Head hanging then, like a sulking child that wished to please but just didn't know how, you took your shamefaced leave of her and hurried off to the dressing room.

The room was divided into several private compartments, each furnished with a closet, a mirror and a chair. Under the chair lay a little gray cardboard suitcase on the cover of which a name was painted in white—surnames all after animals: Fuchs, Wolf, Baer, Loewe; proper names without exception: Israel or Sarah, depending on sex or sexual inclination.

You stripped yourself naked, cast off suit or uniform and all other signs of your public identity, and opened the little suitcase. In it you found the folded essentials of a life: underwear, shirts, pants, glasses, prayer shawl and skullcap—everything humanly imaginable was pressed in, from family photographs to silk stockings and fine lace lingerie, address books, hearing aids, false teeth and real diamonds. Some contents suggested humble means: ragged trousers patched at seat and knees, collarless shirts;

others betokened a lavish life of pearls and perfume. The suitcases were all so realistically packed, you couldn't tell for sure: did they once belong to real people? or had skillful fingers simulated the effect? You didn't ask any questions, but neatly hung up your public persona in the closet and slipped into this strange disguise.—Clothes make the man.

And now you were no longer SS-Oberstgruppenführer Hans Schmidt, but rather Israel Fuchs, furrier from Paris; not Gauleiter Ulrich Gruber, but Israel Baer, watchmaker and crafty intellectual from Krakow. "Fuchs!" screeched a shrill female voice. The door swung open. A strapping blond stood there whip in hand. Every Fuchs had his very own blond. "Down, Fuchs!" she shouted, and the whip cracked menacingly close. "Crawl, Fuchs!" shrieked the blond. And if you were too slow about it, you got a sharp taste of leather on your ass. And the sweet blond siren sang:

> "Fuchs, you scum, you swallowed Schmidt
> Spit him out again, spit him out again
> If you don't, the whip can make you—
> You'll be sorry the-e-en . . .
> If you don't, the whip can make you,
> You'll be sorry then."

You sang along and your own voice sounded strange to you. Your skin smelled different, pungentlike. And the blond bitch suddenly dropped her valkyrie curls. And she was dark on top and down below where you sly Fuchs, you licked her. The whip cracked. "Oy veh! Oy veh!" you heard yourself howling in ecstasy.

Then the lumbering Baer comes sniffing about. "Shalom, Fuchs! What's new? Why are you crying so pitifully?" "Because it hurts, you blockhead!" "Then why let her beat you?" "Because I like it—oy!"

But a Baer wouldn't think of dancing on such thin ice. He'd sooner slip on his spectacles and escape to the library to search out in books what he's too scared to experience directly. He rubs his sweaty paws on his lap and leafs hungrily through forbidden books. In another life he might well have been an enthusiastic follower of the good Dr. Goebbels, one of those idealistic young students who lent a hand in the big book-burning of 1933. What the tongues of fire lapped up that day (books henceforth prohibited in the Reich)—copies of each lay scattered in disorderly heaps on the big round table in Frau Alma's reading room: epitaphs to German literature by the brothers Mann, the two Zweigs, Freud, Einstein, Heine, Remarque, among other sons of the fatherland—with foreign entries by Gorki, Sinclair, London, Proust and the blind Helen Keller.

Baer plucks a volume, a book of stories, out of the heap: A Modern Way to Die by Paul Leopold Wolf, a minor expressionist. He flips the pages and focuses on one passage:

"Life twists like a snake through skyscraper forest and over the cement lawn. Only the barbed wire bush is still in bloom. At last we've conquered nature . . ."

"Decadent trash!" Baer grumbles disappointed, having expected something a little more explicit; he flings the book back into the heap.

"What's your pleasure, sir?" inquires the librarian, a fat cow named Elsa.

"Something satisfying!" Baer grins sheepishly— "Something rapturously realistic!"

"You want stark realism, honey?!" Elsa giggles, "Go look at yourself in the mirror!" And she laughs so hard her ample bosom bursts the confines of its tight bodice and spills out onto the table. Elsa pulls a slender opus out from under her right tit. Baer wipes little sweat beads from his brow, and drooling, scrutinizes book and breast. "Come and get it, sweetie!" she coaxes. Requiring no further enticement, he mounts the table and crawls toward her, scattering modern classics in his path. Panting, he arrives at his delicate destination and grabs for it, but the tit explodes, splattering whitewash all over his troubled countenance. Baer scowls perplexed. Elsa titters. Her breast was a balloon. And she is no she at all, but a regular client, a clown affectionately known as Löwerl—Little Lion, who now dangles the book before Baer's bespectacled chagrin. "What have we here?" chuckles Löwerl. "The perfect punchline!" he wheezes in an asthmatic fit of laughter, reading the title aloud: "*Jokes and their Relation to the Unconscious*—!"

Löwerl, former Minister of Transport, and an authority on the shipment of live cargo, also cherished literature—particularly of the religious kind. He loved to lie at night in the cabinet in Frau Alma's chapel, among the sacred scrolls with their velvet skirts and silver bells. Behind the curtain you could hear him moan. The bells jingled. And when the curtain was pulled back the following morning, worshippers were accustomed to the sight of his hairy legs wrapped

tenderly around the holy parchment, his limp penis pointing to the day's passage.

It was Passover, the Feast of Deliverance, 1945. The Allies
lay in wait outside the ruined city. You heard the approaching thunder, but refused to acknowledge its source.

Everyone sat gathered around the big table, which for
the occasion had been cleared of books and laden with a
vast abundance of food and drink. Reb Baer conducted the
service. Frau Alma sat by in silence.

"This is the bread of affliction that our forefathers ate
in the land of Egypt," Reb Baer read aloud, pointing out
the three wafers of dry flat bread. "Let all who are hungry
come and eat. Let all who are thirsty . . ."

"Kiddush! Kiddush!" Reb Löwerl interrupted—"We
forgot to bless the wine!"

"So we did," Baer conceded, reluctant to admit to his
imperfect mastery of the ritual. He awkwardly rose to his
feet, almost toppling over the bottle of Mouton Cadet
Rothschild '38, and proceeded to pour everyone a glassfull
(including, on Fuchs's prompting, one for the Prophet Elijah, whose arrival to herald the coming of the Messiah is
traditionally expected on this day). Then loudly and un-
melodically he intoned: "Baruch Atah Adonai . . ."

"For God's sake, Baer," Reb Fuchs jabbed him with his
elbow in the gut, "The Lord isn't deaf, you know!"

"Hmmm!" Baer pouted, paused and continued:
"Blessed art Thou, Oh Lord, Our God, King of the Universe,
Who created the fruit of the vine."

"Amen!" all cried in thirsty unison, and raised their
glasses to their lips.

"Wait!" Baer shouted, holding up his hands: "There's
still a second prayer!"

"Get on with it!" Fuchs grumbled.

Baer grinned: "The Lord will have his due." He paused again, belched, then let the words ring out: "Baruch Atah Adonai. Blessed art Thou, Oh Lord, Our God, King of the Universe, Who chose us from among all peoples." Everyone muttered an impatient Amen and downed their first.

Whoever is familiar with the ritual, knows that on this night the righteous must drink four full cups of wine. This pious company drank four times four and soon lost count. The old traditional songs were sung, the one about the little goat and the Angel of Death, and others; the festivities continued far into the night.

So plastered was the merry company that no one even blinked an eye when the little chambermaid suddenly appeared, tiptoed over to Frau Alma and whispered something into her ear. Had anyone among the guests still been sober enough to notice, he would have witnessed an extraordinary, albeit fleeting, transformation in the old woman's otherwise stony expression. Like a dagger-sharp ray of sunlight that cuts through the clouds, strokes the ground and disappears again so soon thereafter that its presence is perceived only as an absence—Frau Alma's eyes narrowed and her mouth bent upwards into the faintest trace of a smile. "We have visitors!" she announced, got up and left the room.

"Must be the Prophet Elijah come for his glass of wine!" Löwerl joked, eliciting a few chuckles.

Seconds later, soldiers of the Red Army, machine gun in hand, stormed into the room, followed by Frau Alma. Some of the stunned celebrants sprung up from their chairs and gaped in terror. Others laughed at this clever joke arranged for their amusement.

"Shalom, Elijah!" Löwerl greeted the officer in charge. "And these, I suppose," he snickered, nodding toward the other soldiers, "are the angels of the Apocalypse!—isn't it so?" he winked at Frau Alma. Her sad eyes registered no response. She raised her hands in the air, rocked slowly back and forth, and like a grieving mother, whispered the prayer for the dead: "Yisgadal Veyishtabach Shemeh Rabah . . ." The machine guns laughed and the bewildered martyrs cried out Amen.

Exquisite Scream, According to X

"Io sentia d'ogni parte trarre guai,
e non vedea persona che 'l facesse."

Here beneath the dark blue boughs, in the white shadow of the midnight sun, X breaks off a branch and he screams, the branch not X. X collects screams. He already has quite a considerable collection and is well known for it. X, it is said, has the most important scream collection in the world. Which is your favorite, a TV interviewer once asked. This one, said X, pulling a dagger out of his briefcase and driving it into the interviewer's heart. The interviewer screamed. But X's dagger was only a toy. The audience laughed relieved. It was just a joke. In fact, X prefers the silent scream. Ants scream so sweetly at the collapse of an anthill. Every scream has its own particular color, X wrote in his book, *The Scream and Its Colors*. The grass screams yellow, not green, beneath the revolving blade of the mower. Ice screams blue when you smash it with a hammer. Children's screams are almost colorless, after lengthy repetition, that is—the newborn invariably screams bright black. X travels a lot and to the remotest places, but his favorite listening site is still a New York fire escape at midnight. It is here that you hear the lovely scream of the disconsolate. Not the crude, coarse, throat-splitting squall so often associated with the purple clatter of dropped bottles. No. Another kind of complaint. A pale blue storming that creeps windlike along the wall. Its source is uncertain. All that is certain is the dull silver clatter on the eardrum. Exquisite, according to X.

Jonah:
A Fish Story

So I go see a specialist to have my lungs looked at because I have trouble breathing.

He glances at the x-ray, ruffles his astute brow, eyes me with concern, then the x-ray again, then me again:

—I'm sorry to tell you this, Mr. W., but you have no lungs at all!

—Come again!?

—You did have them once. (He strains to maintain a reassuring tone.) According to the x-ray, the cavity is still there, but the lungs aren't. Are you sure you didn't have them removed by mistake?

—Quite sure.

—Now don't get upset. (He smiles uncomfortably.) There's always a scientific explanation. Let's have a listen, shall we?

I remove my shirt and the doctor raises his stethoscope, about to lay its cold ear against my back to monitor my breathing, when I hear a gasp of extended duration.

—What is it, Doctor! (I cry out, concerned at that moment more for his sake than for mine.)

—I don't know how to tell you this (he says, placing one hand on his heaving chest and the other on his uncontrollably twitching brow), you're growing gills.

—Gills?! (I say.)

—Gills (he nods), definitely gills.

—Are you sure it isn't an . . . allegoric reaction?

—Quite sure. I've never seen anything like it. (He sighs, sinking into expensive padded leather.)

My utter faith in the miracles of modern medicine notwithstanding, I am beginning to get worried.

—Tell me, Doctor, what should I do!

He shakes his head:

—I can only suggest that you proceed immediately to the nearest pet shop and buy yourself the biggest fish tank you can find.

—You mean (I say, having prepared myself for the worst, a transplant or permanent attachment to an iron lung), I should go swimming?

—Precisely, and there's no time to lose! Call me if you have any further complications though in the future, quite frankly, I would recommend that you consult a veterinarian or a marine biologist. My secretary will send you the bill.

—Thanks, Doc (I say, somewhat dismayed).

So I hurry home, oblivious to the midday procession of suffering humanity—Don't I have my own troubles to worry about!—and as the jingle says, I let my fingers do the walking. I call up every pet shot in town. No luck. Nobody has a tank big enough to fit me. But I don't despair. Necessity is the mother of contention, or something like that. I turn to the section in the Yellow Pages that says "Swimming Pool Contractors, Dirs. & Designers," and dial the first listing.

—Aquatics Plus (says an audibly platinum blond re-cording). We do in-ground and above-ground, commercial and residential installations—Please hold!

I hold.

Finally:

—Aquatics Plus, Marjorie speaking, how can I help you?

—I need a pool installed (I say) how long will it take?

—That depends on the terrain (she says), earth, sand or stone?

—Linoleum (I reply).

—Come again!?

—Linoleum (I repeat), probably over parquet though I've never been inclined to look. I'm not the home repair type.

—Sorry (she says), I have no interior experience. You'll have to speak to the manager, Mr. Schwimmer—hold please!

I hold.

At last:

—Sidney Schwimmer here, that means nautalist, in case you didn't know.

—I didn't.

—I know what you're thinking (says Sidney Schwim-mer), everybody thinks I made it up to boost business, well I didn't, some names are just prophetic, I read in *Life* about a sex therapist named Dr. Love.

—About the pool! (I cut him short.)

—The pool, yes (he says, audibly balding). I under-stand you're interested in an urban interior.

—Yes.

—Have you considered a hot tub?

—It's got to be big (I insist).

—Two's a party, three's an orgy, huh! (says Sidney

Schwimmer, his inflection figuratively jabbing an elbow into my ribs). And I'll throw in a whirlpool at no extra charge.

—No whirlpool, thanks (I say).

—It's a package deal (he insists), every tub comes with a whirlpool at our one low low price.

—Okay (I say), I'll take the whirlpool. When can you install?

—Well (he says), we're a little backed up just now, what with the summer months hot on our heels and the temperature scheduled to reach a record high.

—When?

—Did you know that hundreds died of heat frustration in Greece and Turkey last summer, which caused quite a stir in Massapequa!

—When!

—Well (he calculates mentally), barring a threatened strike by the installation men—Damn unions are practically driving us out of business! What do they care about suffering suburbia! All they know is time off and overtime! Asiatics know how to work though, lemme tell ya, that's how come the Koreans are cornering the world aquatics market.

—When!?! (I shriek, my patience expired.)

—Well (he says, clearing his throat), I'd say we could have the job done three weeks to six months after we start, that's after the plumbers take a look at your pipes, of course, and the building inspector gives the go-ahead, which sometimes, to be perfectly frank, can take time unless you're willing to grease the municipal palm, if you catch my meaning.

—Can't you be any more precise than that?

—I sympathize with your plight, believe me (says Sidney Schwimmer), I know what it means to sweat! But I can tell you this, Trusty Tubs in Syosset won't do it any quicker.

—Thanks (I say curtly and hang up).

It being the dead of winter, a dip in the ocean is hardly an option.

I have one last resort.

Wheezing, gasping, sucking for air, I arrive at the entrance to the New York Aquarium at Coney Island.

The place is deserted. I bang, I knock, I rattle the metal door till an irate custodian appears.

—Sorry, son (he says), we're closed for renovations.

—It's an emergency! (I insist.)

—Most people go under the boardwalk (he suggests).

—Not that kind of an emergency (I say), I *have* to get in!

—Listen, pal (he says), the place is closed! chiuso! cerrado! varmacht! in case you don't understand plain English.

—You have to let me in! It's my last hope! (I plead.)

—What are you, some kind o' psycho or somethin'! So you'll see the killer sharks when we re-open in May!

—Now!!! (I gasp, hardly still able to formulate words.)

—You wanna see fish? Go to the Fulton Fish Market, they got fish! Honestly, I don't know what's a matter wit' you kids nowadays wit' yer Jaws I, II, III! Must be all that raw fish you eat! You got vicious imaginations!

Desperation gets the better of me.

I pick up a faded COME TO THE AQUARIUM FOR A WHALE OF A GOOD TIME sign with a smiling blue leviathan.

—I'm sorry (I whisper, not being violent by nature, and

strike the custodian from behind just as he turns to shut the door in my face). I race into the dark dank interior, past empty tank after tank. The plaques are still in place identifying the various species of absent sea life by their unpronounceable Latin names and Anglo-Saxon equivalents: Anarrhichthys Ocellatus (Wolf Eel), Haemulon Flavolineatum Pomadasyidae (French Grunt), Myripristis Jacobus Holocentripidae (Blackbar Soldierfish). The names are there but no water and no fish. Finally I spot a single mammoth tank far to the rear still filled with mirky H_2O. I have no choice. There's a ladder lying around. I drag it over, prop it against the glass wall, and before I can have any second thoughts I'm up and over the edge.

Relief at last!

It is as if the air in its thin insufficiency never really suited my respiratory needs. For here I feel suddenly at home as never before. I am in my element. I can breathe easy. I tear off my clothes, strip down to my waterproof watch and do flip-flops for joy. True, the water is filthy and I can barely see a nautical inch in front of my eyes, but what are the relative disagreeability and possible long-term health hazards of a little pollution compared to the imminent threat of suffocation!

It is the bubbles that alarm me. Big black bubbles. Bubbles the size of my head rising from below. I sense them rather than see them, feel them spread their aqueous film around me before bursting in the air above.

Stay calm! I tell myself, it might be a motor. That's it, of course, it's a motor! Fish tanks have water pumps and water pumps have motors. The filter's a little clogged up with silt, that's all. Best to ignore it, I decide, which is my general policy when it comes to mechanical malfunction. Let the problem repair itself.

You know how unnerving a leaky faucet can get.

The slow incessant drops, hardly audible at first, then little by little they get louder and louder till the swelling sound coopts consciousness and you can think of nothing else. And soon it is like the roar of boulders falling, a slow-motion underwater avalanche an inch away from my ear.

Now imagine that noise magnified a hundredfold and the drops all the more massive, only the faucet is upside-down and the drops are introverted bubbles of air rising instead of falling and you yourself are the reluctant drain.

Fed up at last, upset to the point of action, I take a precipitous nose dive, but the surface I strike is neither metallic nor plastic, as I had expected. It is far too bouncy, too resilient.

Blubber! I conclude with a cold shudder.

Now the water is churning beneath me. The bubbles multiply. Great waves are sweeping me in their wake, and now I am quite certain that the source of this upheaval is of natural origin.

I will go on speaking though I know that my life is a gulp away from extinction. Never, alas! will they accord me a Latin name and encompass me in the nomenclature of acknowledged being. No zooanatomist will dissect me to study my bone structure. No marine biologist will examine my mating habits. No Neodarwinian will recognize the implications of my mutation as a bold step backwards, an anatomical regression to antedeluvial bliss.

Minutes pass, hours perhaps. Time as such hardly matters here, though my trusty Timex is still ticking. I could count the bubbles, but what difference would it make? Their pattern is unpredictable, irregular, and—dare I say it?—almost human. The one fact I have to cling to is the fact that I am still here, have not yet been (though I might at any moment be) engulfed by invisible jaws. Panic dissolves into anguish, anguish into annoyance, annoyance into malaise, malaise diluted into a watery tincture of boredom. I would drown myself if I hadn't already done so. My thinking is slow, positively piscine. A last idea scuttles the reef of reason. If drowning is out, then why not attempt a selachian suicide? Bob back up to the surface and suffocate forthrightly on the fringe of my old airy habitat!

Once, twice I try it, but my limbs fail to propel me with sufficient force. A third time I barely manage to rise to ear-level before gravity reasserts itself.

Yet there is one small consolation. An aural mirage perhaps, the fata morgana of a desperate fish, but I could swear I heard decipherable syllables, intelligible sounds emerging from the pop of the black bubbles.

I surge upwards again with renewed purpose, and this time I am quite certain of it: the bubbles burst into words. For I distinctly heard a sputtered: HELLO, HANDSOME! before I sank.

Additional lunges enable me to reconstitute the following message:

MY NAME IS DASCYLLUS ARUANUS POMACENTRI-PIDAE, BUT YOU CAN CALL ME THREE-STRIPED DAMSELFISH.

A memory flash:

I had these two goldfish when I was a kid, a male and a female. And late at night when everyone was asleep I took a flashlight and shined it on the tank. Uninformed yet dying to know, I kept waiting for a third little fish to appear, wondering where it might come from. And then one morning I approached the tank and noticed that there was only one fish left and a severed tail floating suspiciously in its wake. 1 + 1 = 1 (a mathematical enigma). Is that how they do it? I wondered.

And wonder even now, feeling at my nethermost parts the first hungry nibble of love.

The Human Butterfly

I am the human butterfly with wings of glass. I was a baby caterpillar once. Then I found myself crawling into bed beside a man and a woman. I slipped inside the woman and when the man couldn't fit, he yelled, "Marie, what you got in there?"

"Why nothing, Henry dear," she whispered oh so romantically, fake eyelashes fluttering.

"Don't tell me *nothing*! You got something hid in there and I wanna know *what*!"

So Marie, who does feel a bit funny—though delighted, nonetheless, to have me as a boarder in there, so to speak—pokes her finger in and she says, "My Henry dear, you're right! There is something in there and it's *alive*!"

"Well what the hell is it?"

"I don't know, Henry, feels something like a caterpillar."

(It is important to note that Henry and Marie are quite

young in fact, little over five and a half, but advanced for their tender years, as children are these days.)

Well Henry, who's getting mad thinking some other boy left his thing in there for Marie to play with, and doesn't believe a word about birds, bees or caterpillars, pokes around, sticks his finger in and pulls me out.

(Meanwhile, I was sleeping soundly, dreaming such dreams!—of being born a human.

"So the cocoon isn't good enough for you, you lazy good-for-nothing," my mother scolds.

"But I don't feel like a caterpillar!"

"Just you wait. You'll see. *They'll* tell you what you are. They'll let you know you're nothing but a lousy caterpillar.")

And while I floated amidst human dreams of grandeur, Henry goes and pulls me out of Marie and he asks me what I am—though in the dream it's a caterpillar cop doing the asking, waving a twig club over my head.

"Why I'm a human caterpillar—what else?" And I look myself over to disprove my dreamed-up lie, and there I am with furry hands and feet just like a man, only with the slinky snake body of a caterpillar.

"This must be our child!" Marie moans with delight, grabbing me and pressing me to her unripe breast. "Now let's play house, Henry. You're the Daddy and I'll be the Mommy and this here skinny little worm will be our baby."

Henry, who only wants to please, goes along with the game. "How's my honey?" he grins like a middle-aged man just home from the office to his wife.

"I'm just fine!" Marie smiles. "Now kiss baby caterpillar. Baby *loves* Daddy!"

So Henry, despite obvious disgust, bends over to kiss me, but I, being so scared, and thinking for sure that Henry has every intention of swallowing me, dive right back in between Marie's legs.

And when I came out again I was a human butterfly for real. With wings of glass and a rush of desires that I could neither understand nor satisfy. And I flew out the window and into your fields. And when you see a butterfly, look twice! He may have a human face and a worried look just like your own.

The Tale of
the Louse

The louse lived contentedly atop the old man's bald head. Since the man was indeed very old, and since he seldom moved other than to shift from side to side in bed and turn the pages of a book, the louse enjoyed a life of absolute leisure. So carefree was his existence, so boring at times, that he began to wonder what it was like to live as others do—running, jumping, ever fleeing from the tireless fingernails of fate.

When things got dreary on the slick surface of the nearly bald pate, the louse would wander down the furrows of a wrinkled brow to the old man's eyes, where for fun, he might dangle from a lash, or roll over the aquiline peak of the nose, and languish in a dark, damp nostril where a warm breeze was forever blowing.

And on those rare occasions when relatives came to visit, he liked to take them on a tour of the estate, to show off every stiff joint and acrid smelling orifice—oh how they groaned with envy!

*   *   *

One night the old man could not sleep. He tossed and turned, and in the morning he reached for his teeth that had been soaking in a glass of greenish water for as long as the louse could remember. An unprecedented gesture. Then the shaky hand set out again, this time to scour the netherregions between bed and floorboard, unearthing a pair of mouldy leather artifacts. What next? thought the louse with a curiosity that bordered on anxiety—as rusty bedsprings creaked, dust clouds lifted and slowly, ever so arduously, the old man sat up—and did what he had never done: he scratched his head. And though the finger missed its mark, the louse cried out in terror.

There followed a flurry of frightening new sensations: the cold slap of water, the foul smell of soap, and when the old man went so far as to brush his five or six hairs, the louse leaped for his life, barely escaping being malled by the deadly bristles.

Enough! pleaded the louse, having had his fill of excitement for a lifetime—but the cataclysmic outburst of activity continued.

Now fully dressed, the old man picked up an old straw basket, shook out its rodent squatters and placed it upside down on his head. Then he grabbed hold of a silver-tipped, black ebony cane and hobbled to the door. Frightened by the jingle of keys, the louse burrowed his way deep into the wax of a hairy ear canal, from the shelter of which he hoped to safely oversee all further developments.

And then the door opened, and with a gust of wind and a cacophany of voices, the wide world rudely introduced itself. From the tousled heads of street urchins and the blankets of beggars, from the pelts of mangy dogs, from every window and doorway came the crazed howl of his demented brethren—overcome as he was by pity and horror at their miserable plight, the louse passed out.

In the shadow of a doorway he came to again. The sign said: Mortimer Adler, M.D. Home at last, thought the louse in a delusion of relief, for although quite adept at deciphering print from all the books the old man read, he had never learned its meaning. The old man knocked and a moment later the door swung open.—How do you do, Mr. Altman? said a soft voice from inside.

Barely recovered from the deafening ordeal of the street, the poor louse was once again overwhelmed. There stood a creature dressed all in white. It resembled the old man in essential form and structure and yet it was altogether different. Its presence seemed to overflow into the space around it, so that one could not say for sure where it ended and the room began. The old man was likewise powerfully affected, his knees gave way beneath him and he had to be led to a couch.—Mr. Altman! Mr. Altman!? Vibrations shook the louse's lair, long brown strands of hair brushed up against it, and a sweet scent thrilled his senses. Oh how the louse longed to leap! And would have done so at that instant, were its little legs not paralyzed by a furious agitation.—Mr. Altman, the voice whispered close up to the old man's ear, the doctor will see you now.

The room was all white. Mirrors, shining metal objects and jarring bright lights were suspended from ceiling and walls.

Everything reeked of disinfectant.—How do you feel, Mr. Altman? said a short, fat, balding creature not unlike the old man in appearance, though he lacked the potato-like smell of old age. The latter extracted a tube of light from a breast pocket and shone it first into the old man's eyes and then into each ear. And when the light struck, illuminating the cavernous hollow, a huge black creature (something like a giant louse) lunged forward from the far wall of the inner ear—at which the poor little louse took fright and jumped over the precipice into the pupil of a squinting eye.

Thus separated for the first time from his former host, lodged, so to speak, in the eye of the beholder, and stunned by his sudden isolation, he examined every corner and crevice of the body he had once called home.—Is it serious, doctor? asked the old man.—Serious indeed! Why you'll outlive us all! the other laughed. And then with longing, nostalgia, and a deep sense of loss, the louse watched his old carefree existence get up and disappear out the door.

His new host washed his hands.—Nurse, he called, is there anyone else?—No one but me! said the creature in white, leaning in the doorway, spilling her scent. An eye blinked. A hand wiped away a tear of lust. So ends the tale of the louse.

It

Unravelled it would span a hundred city blocks, climb the emergency steps up both World Trade Center towers and still have the length left for a leisurely stroll around the circumference of New York's Central Park.

Archeologists from the University of Nevada team studying it have not yet been able to ascertain what it is.

The item in question, a tube composed of the small intestines of a prehistoric species of sheep sewn together and decorated with human earlobes, was unearthed by construction crews digging the foundation of the Underama Palace, Las Vegas's first underground nuclearproof resort hotel, projected for completion in the year 2000.

It's one hell of a big hose is what it is, the foreman on duty, Matt Drury, reported. We didn't know what to do with it, so we notified the folks at the university. They always know what to do with things you don't know what to do with.

*   *   *

Professor Waldemar Jenkins, who was called in as an expert, and who has helped identify innumerable obscure finds in construction sites around the world (most notably, the viper skin prophylactics employed by ancient Egyptian mummifiers afraid of the afterlife consequences of their necrophile tendencies) told reporters at a press conference that the object was still under scrutiny. Based on analysis completed to date, Professor Jenkins added, all that can be said for certain is that we don't know what it is, or was.

In a paper delivered to the Annual Conference of Arcane Discoveries (CAD), Professor Jenkins elaborated further:

It is my great pleasure to report to you, ladies and gentlemen, fellow scholars and students of the arcane, on our tentative findings concerning the identity and purpose of an object which has in recent months received a great deal of attention in the media, a tube of considerable length composed of animal matter, conclusively dated as a pre-Ice Age specimen, which my fellow investigators and I on the University of Nevada team have tentatively labeled the "Underama" Tube.

Thanks to the generosity and foresight of investors in Underama Palace, on the site of which, as you know, the tube was discovered, it is being stored in a temperature- and humidity-controled chamber the size of a football field pending an official government decision on what to do with it.

As to the object's identity, my colleagues and I have conflicting theories, the thrust of which I would like to present to you today in the hope that it may help us to unravel the mystery.

Dr. Horace Greenspan (whose astute analysis of pre-Colombian pipelines presented in a paper delivered to this very society some years ago offered what to my mind is a convincing challenge to the established premise that pipes are a modern, that is to say, historic invention) believes the "Underama" Tube to be a kind of primitive pipeline that stretched in antediluvial times from the lake that was the Painted Desert to the sea that filled Death Valley.

Dr. Helen Walters takes issue with Dr. Greenspan's hypothesis. It is the presence of human earlobes, according to Dr. Walters, that discounts the pipeline theory. Dr. Walters, a specialist in oracular relics, author of the highly acclaimed, if controversial, study of the Oedipus legend, "What If Oedipus Was Impotent?", sees the earlobes as evidence of oracular purpose. Earlobes and foreskins, Dr. Walters maintains, were favored fertility fetishes throughout the ancient world. It is Dr. Walters's contention that the "Underama" Tube was employed by its creators as a vast symbolic fallopian tube running from the womb of Mother Earth, a temple cave located at the Underama Palace construction site, to the great vaginal lip, a hot spring that once spouted in downtown Reno.

As a third, and equally intriguing possibility, let me offer the opinion of my learned colleague, Dr. Suliman Ibn Bradford, Professor of Archeological Anatomy on leave from Old Dominion University, in Roanoke, Virginia. Animal intestines, according to Dr. Ibn Bradford, are still considered by certain tribal shamans among the Eskimos as an effective purgative when filled with hot water and wrapped around the afflicted subject's middle. In Eskimo mythology, the intestines of the primeval seal were cut out by the Great Hunter, ancestor of the modern Eskimo, and cast upon the water to still the ache of Mother Ocean after giving birth to the world.

With all due respect to Dr. Ibn Bradford's compelling, might I say daring, ideas, we must remind him that Nevada is after all quite a distance from Alaska, and that seals have never been known to thrive in the desert.

Having summarized the views of my revered colleagues, let me no longer try your patience, ladies and gentlemen, and proceed immediately to my own theory.

It is my belief, though I may very well be wrong, that the "Underama" Tube had no purpose at all, and that it was created over generations by a society much like our own with abundant time on its hands and nothing better to do.

Why must everything that pre-historic man did have a purpose? Surely he had as much a right to unreasoned activity as we. Where better than here in Las Vegas do we know the lengths man will go to amuse himself, and enliven his idle hours! For the roulette wheel is only another form of the clock, and the slot machine a standby for staring into the void.

I humbly suggest, ladies and gentlemen, that the vast tube unearthed at the Underama construction site was fashioned by our ancestors to soothe their primordial ennui.

Why animal intestines? Why human earlobes?

Why do old men sit on porches whittling sticks? Why do young men already rich enough to retire on the interest of their millions invest in underground pleasure domes? And why, my learned friends, do we scholars of the ancient stare at broken dishes and rusty nails, and listen to the ruminations of a doddering academic on the identity of a refrigerated accumulation of prehistoric slop?

Because we, just like our worthy ancestors, have nothing better to do . . . Professor Jenkins's remarks caused quite a stir in the scholarly community; some experts in the field went so far as to suggest the onset of senility. The debate over the tube rages on.

Meanwhile, as a token of their sense of civic responsibility, the board of directors of Underama, Inc., on behalf of all Underama investors, decided to donate the tube and its protective shelter to the State of Nevada. Plans are underway to license public viewing.

And one young couple from California has already applied to be married at the mouth of the tube. Professional interest, claims the future groom, a broker in pork bellies.

Lovey and Me

My hacienda straddles the platform. It is constructed of spittle and swiss cheese aged to a rock-hard finish. In it live Lovey and me.

Lovey, I say, what's on your mind today? It's drafty in our villa, she says, calling it a villa even though I have tried to convince her of its hacienda-like south-of-the-border character. It's windy, Lovey, I say, because of the holes. Plug 'em up, she replies. Oh no, I couldn't, it's in the nature of solid swiss cheese finish to preserve and proudly display its holes. Don't you want the neighbors to envy us, Lovey?

In the place I lived with Herb I never felt chilly.

No, I said, of course not, what sand castle ever allowed the wind to blow through its bedrooms, but I'll bet it got awfully wet sometimes!

Oh yes, it did, she admitted, the waves kept banging against the walls, eroding our sense of security. Isn't it wonderful, Herb used to say, Don't you just love the sound of waves? He was a lot like you, come to think of it. No, Herb, I said, I don't. I couldn't sleep for worrying.

Portals, Lovey, I said, that's what I like about our hacienda, our windows are like portals; it's like a boat, only anchored.

Every day Herb and I would have to heap sand to buttress the collapsing walls of our castle. One day, Herb, I said, one day I won't dig with you any more. Don't you just love our little sandcrabs, Darling? he'd say. He called me Darling.

I call you Lovey.

I know, but Herb called me Darling.

Do you want me to call you Darling, Lovey?

Oh no, it wouldn't be natural!

Toast me a grilled wall sandwich, will you!

Toast it yourself!

What's the matter, Lovey?

Herb always wanted me to make his sandcakes and with you it's your grilled wall sandwiches.

That's just one more advantage of living in a hacienda built out of edible parts, I was quick to point out.

Herb never ate the cakes I made him.

Herb didn't appreciate you like I do, Lovey.

In his fashion he did.

How often did he do it with you, Lovey, tell me that!

Often enough, she said, often enough.—This villa is claustrophobic!

How can you say that? How can you call our hacienda claustrophobic?

Why, I wonder, she said, do I always take up with homebodies? Why are all the men in my life nuts about their domiciles? You never take me dancing, you never take me to the movies!

Who needs the movies, Lovey, when you can just peer out our portals, every one of them set at a different angle, each perspective unique!

Herb said pretty much the same about the sound of waves. He said I couldn't appreciate the accoustic subtleties. I wore earplugs for a while, then I left him.

Come here, get a load of this, Lovey.—There's a man taking notes on our way of life.

Where?

There!

I'm leaving, she said just like that, I'm going with the man even if I have to live the rest of my life in a notebook.

Garbage

"Garbage!—it's all you're good for's bringing garbage home," Mrs. Barnes said to her husband. "Yeah, I know," he muttered, examining the shell of an old radio.

"Listen to me! Why don't you listen!?" she complained. "Where am I gonna put it?" But he had already scooped up the brown box, cradled it under his arm and walked on ahead. She followed him reluctantly. In front of every promising heap he paused like a dog sniffing out familiar scents. And every time he bent down to consider a find, she groaned: "Garbage!" But he wasn't listening. Some secret project was ever in the process of taking shape in his mind, lacking only this one last ingredient.

Habit enslaves. Mrs. Barnes hated her husband, had hated him with a passionate constancy for all the thirty years of their marriage, hated him the way a woman can hate only a man she can no longer do without. Years ago she had contemplated leaving him, but fear stood guard at the front door and somehow the suitcases never got packed.

To Mr. Barnes, his wife was just an irksome screech in the machinery, one that needed oiling from time to time but could otherwise be ignored—while in the garage, his true love, the Project, grew month by month, year by year, until the four walls were no longer large enough to hold it and one of them had to be knocked down.

"I can't take it anymore! I'm leaving!" she snarled every morning over breakfast. He nodded, knowing full well that though she once may have meant it, the daily harangue had long since become ritual. "You spend more time in that damn garage than you ever did with me," she growled. "Uh-huh!" he mumbled, gulped down his coffee and disappeared.

One night she had had enough. It was either the thing in the garage or her, and she meant to win.

It wasn't jealousy that drove her, or the desire to regain his love. His hairy flaccid figure disgusted her every time he came near, and she knew that the feeling was mutual. Her fallen breasts and sagging belly—the result of five miscarriages—even made her feel queezy on the rare occasions when she accidentally caught a glimpse of herself in the hallway mirror.

She waited till she heard his snoring, then slipped out of bed and put on the once pink, now grimy gray dressing gown he'd given her on their second wedding anniversary, the last one they'd celebrated. It was a full moon out. She snickered at the romantic connotations.

* * *

Meanwhile, Mr. Barnes lay dreaming of his design. It contained the sum total of his life's endeavor. A retired garbage man (or sanitation engineer, as the young ones like to call themselves nowadays), he had never much succeeded at anything else: not at auto repairs, not as a wrecker, not as a husband. It was his life's ambition to be a great inventor though he'd have been hard pressed to say what exactly he was attempting to invent. Now he dreamt that he flicked a switch and the thing came alive. It squeaked and trembled and then it started rolling slowly out through where the fourth garage wall had been. A faint smile ruffled the pattern of his wrinkles. Happiness drooled out the side of his mouth and soaked the pillow like when he was a boy.

"It works!" he cried, "Honey, come look! It works!"

She walked toward him in the dream, and for the first time in years he felt a flicker of love. She was smiling, holding something behind her back, but he couldn't tell what. She moved mechanically forward and raised a hammer above her head. And then it was not she who held the hammer, but *it* approaching her, and his wife was the thing on wheels rolling out of the garage. He watched in horror mixed with wonder as the thing brought the hammer down on her head.

Mr. Barnes woke to the crash. He reached beside him and felt the cold sheet where the blanket had been pulled back. He jumped into his pants and rushed out.

Still bent over it by the time he got there, she kept hacking in a frenzy. Seconds passed till she became aware of his presence. She looked up, grinned and started laughing hysterically. "Our baby!" she laughed, dipping her hands into the debris, picking up shattered pieces.

He looked back expressionless, the wrinkles restored to order. Her nightgown hung open. The sweat of ecstasy dripped from her forehead and down her neck and the moon shone on her withered breasts.

Limo

The big black limo rounded the corner at 47th and Fifth and for the seventh time in the last fifteen minutes, rolled slowly down the block. Though puzzled and curious, its driver, Sanford Stevens, hired that very day from the ranks of Collin's Executive Car Service, knew better than to ask any questions. He did his job and got paid for it. In the thirty-five years plus of his driving career he had had a lot of peculiar clients, but a dark pane of glass always separated him from his charge and he liked it that way. There was the banker whom he picked up every Thursday evening at 6:30 sharp and dropped off in the Rambles in Central Park, where men seek the embrace of anonymous biceps. And the aging movie star, her face always veiled, whom he picked up with her poodle, drove to a quiet spot where she opened the door and let her dog out to do his business, and then he drove her home again. He had driven the consul of an Arab emirate who was partial to whiskey and adolescents of either sex, and of course, there had been the usual string of ordinary pin-striped executives, determined men who count time by dollars lost.

Again! said the voice on the intercom, once Sanford reached the corner, and so he swung the car around for another spin. Again! the voice insisted, and Again!—Sanford lost count.

By midnight, after three hours of nonstop circling, Sanford was starting to feel the effects, but he had been hired for the whole night and a job was a job. By 1 A.M. he felt dizzy, and ten minutes later he practically welcomed the sound of a police siren behind him and the voice on the loudspeaker telling him to pull over.

Alright, Mr. Merry-go-round, said the patrolman, What's the story!

I don't know, Sanford replied, the world still spinning around him.

I've been watching you, the cop accused: You circled this corner 99 times before I lost count!

I do what I'm told, Sanford explained, nodding toward the speaker over his head.

The officer rapped with his knuckles on the glass.— Open up! he demanded. Open up, I said! But the window didn't roll down. He turned back to the driver: You tell him to open up in there!

Can't.

Why not!? the cop was fuming.

It is a one-way intercom. They talks, I listen.

Can't you signal him?

Nope. One-way communication, that's what the customers want.

Is he a bigwig, a senator, ambassador or something?

the policeman worried in a suddenly respectful whisper, wary lest the incident stir up unpleasant repercussions back at the precinct.

Dunno, Sanford shrugged.

Well, said the patrolman, I guess there's no law against circling.

I guess there ain't.

See that you run no red lights!

Don't plan to.

By 2 A.M. the limo was still circling the same corner. This is sure peculiar, Sanford said to himself.

Again! the voice said, and Again!

Sanford switched on the car radio.

It was one of those talk shows where listeners call in and ask questions.

Go ahead, the announcer said, you're on the air!

I'm a nightwatchman, said the caller, I work long hours.

So what about it!? the announcer rudely replied.

I'm not a drinking man, the caller protested defensively, though I may take a nip every now and then just like the next fellow.

I don't give a damn about your drinking problem— Get to the point! the announcer snarled with insomniac ire. Do you have any questions?

Well, yes, said the caller, That's why I called. There's this car, see, a stretch limo, and it's been circling round the block outside.

So!?

Been circling ever since I started my shift, which was over six hours ago, and I wanna know why.

What do you want *me* to do about it?! the announcer lashed out.

Couldn't you ask him, the driver, I mean? Couldn't you ask him why? the called asked timidly.

Alright, the announcer agreed, for a lark, if only to get rid of the caller. Why not, he said, and clearing his throat: Heh you out there! Whoever the hell you are driving that car round and round the same block—if you're listening, call in and tell us what you're up to, long as it isn't illicit! . . . And now a word from our sponsor. Folks, if you can't sleep nights . . .

Sanford reached for his radio phone. He was only author- ized to use it to call the home office, or in case of emer- gency, but boredom and dizziness outweighed propriety.

He dialed, waited six dial tones and was about to hang up, when he heard the sound of the receiver being lifted.

Hello, NIGHTWATCH, this is Gary Green, you're on the air!

This is Sanford, Sanford Stevens, Sanford said, de- lighted to hear himself on the radio, hoping his fellow drivers were tuned in.

Switch off your radio, for heaven's sake! the announcer yelled.

Disappointed, Sanford complied.

Now what can I do for you? the announcer inquired.

I'm the driver, Sanford replied, basking in the auditory spotlight.

The *what*?

The *driver*!

What do you want, a medal! Why don't you try out for the Indianapolis 500 or maybe the Grand Prix!

The driver, Sanford insisted, of the circling limo.

So you're the mystery man at the wheel! So what's the scoop, Sam?

It's Sanford, Sanford Stevens.

Alright pal, tell the listeners why you keep circling round the same damn block!

I dunno, Sanford had to admit, embarrassed now that he realized he was expected to offer an explanation and that he had none to offer.

How's that?

I just follows my instructions, Sanford muttered, I never asks 'em why.

Well there you have it, ladies and gentlemen, fellow insomniacs, vampires, peeping toms and other creatures of the night, the announcer snickered, and I hope you're satisfied. The mystery driver is just following orders. Just like you 'n me 'n a million other chumps with their foot on the accelerator and their mind on automatic going no-where fast. Remember, you heard it on NIGHTWATCH!

Damn radio!—Sanford hung up.

At 3:45 A.M. the car was still circling around the block. Again! said the voice on the intercom.—Again!

Little Accidents
Will Happen

We are improving it, said the machinist.

At first we had to input what to expel: set its circuits, feed in the data, program the desired response. Now it does it all by itself, and what's more, it is user-friendly, sympathetic in a mechanical sense.

Take the subway, for instance, he said. What would you eliminate if you could without impeding service?

The shriek? The filth? The stench?

The rejector does all that and more. It puts itself in your shoes.

Sometimes, though, it works too well.

Just yesterday, he recalled, stroking the precious device (a spherical structure the size of a beach ball that hummed and sputtered as he spoke).

At Times Square, much to my regret, the attractive secretary seated beside me—whose eyebrows were per-haps a little bushy and thighs a little thick, but the rejector could have taken care of that—she got up and a junior executive inserted himself in her place.

Our mutual dislike was immediate, so thick between us, you could—forgive the cliche!—have cut it with a butter knife. As the train pulled out, the rejector happened to roll onto the man's knee and he removed it. It was the manner in which he did so rather than the fact of his having done it, the overt acrimony in his gesture that offended. The rejector picked up on it too and proceeded to remove his hand, eliminate it, not bloodily but with a surgical expertise. Laserlike. You couldn't tell it had ever been there. Still the man knew something was missing though he was unable to put his finger on quite what it was. Nonchalantly at first, affecting a cool indifference, he cast a covert eye about and fixed on me the way one might on a pickpocket caught in flagrante delicto; he was about to tap his pants pocket to confirm the absence of the familiar bulge of his wallet when the realization struck home that the hand itself was missing. Incredulous, he shook the fallow sleeve, and when with repeated shaking the fingers still failed to emerge the young man lost his painstakingly acquired executive control and, reduced to tears, stamped his feet in a pin-striped temper tantrum.

A mistake, under the circumstances, the machinist pointed out: Electronic annoyance is often unpredictable.

Next thing you know, his fleecy limbs were patting the floor like bedroom slippers. The feet were gone and the stumps struck with a childish futility.

The poor wretch could simply not believe his eyes.

What the hell are you doing!? he said, finally fathoming the loss.

It isn't me, I tried to explain, it's just that you offended my machine.

His mouth fell open, with apoplectic fury and saliva. The rejector more than likely feared his rabid bite. Snap! Gone was the jaw, and the half moon of his upper lip waned into a pathetic crescent, a terrible inextinguishable smile.

As with the reckless disregard of a gambler on a losing streak unable to stop—he could at least have cut his losses—his anger refused to abate; fury shifted to its last expressive outpost, the nostrils, where it flared up, huffed and snarled like a pit bull on a short leash.

Gone the nose.

You can guess the rest.

Organ by organ, my fellow passenger was excised from the picture, and though I sympathized as one human to another, I cannot say that I regretted his disappearance. He brought it on himself.

I too, as you may have noticed, am missing parts, the machinist pointed out.

On close examination, it did indeed become apparent that he was outfitted with a host of prosthetic devices, that he was gently fondling the temperamental ball in his lap with the aid of a mechanical hand, and that the very knees on which it rested though swathed in blue denim, revealed the brittle stiffness of plastic.

The rejector is not to blame, he was quick to add with a nervous grin, little accidents will happen.

The Eye of
the Beholder

". . . time, observation, the sagacity of astronomers, and diligent research may carry
us much farther than we are apt to imagine."

—Johann Heinrich Lambert

Thomas Krampf, a reclusive middle-aged bachelor,
lived alone with his invalid mother.

An avid star gazer of monumental girth and limited
mobility, he took a more than casual interest in the shape
and disposition of the universe.

He particularly liked to point his telescope at a con-
stellation he himself had discovered and duly named Milky
Way II, a cluster of windows in the withered facade of the
Hotel Beauregard across the street, where transient females
were wont to display their assets on warm summer nights.

Also a collector of antique puppets (his prize possession being a Victorian Punch 'n Judy show, complete with
miniature stage, red velvet curtain and a wealth of tiny

paraphernalia), he conceived and performed his own puppet plays, in which he parleyed all the parts, and of which he was the sole spectator.

In "Stargazing" (a favorite in Krampf's repertoire) Punch played the astronomer Galileo. Resplendent in Renaissance cloak and cap, wielding a tiny telescope, riding the puppeteer's right hand, he spots and engages in dialogue with Judy, the North Star, who, sheerly attired in allegorical minimum, graces the puppeteer's left.

Krampf did a compelling falsetto, as his left hand wove through sinuous twists and turns.

The scenario, largely improvised, varied in length and elaboration depending on the mood and inclination of the spellbound audience of one.

The dialogue was far from Platonic:

North Star. There is nothing quite as stimulating as the face of an imagined man. A light in a distant window. His telescope trained on me. Fat or skinny, tall or short, I can make him be anything I like. Sometimes I like to picture an ugly man feasting his eyes on me, a hunchback or a dwarf.

Galileo. You have very esoteric tastes.

North Star. The gaze of an ugly man is so much more piercing, deep and desperate.

Galileo. Indeed.

At this point, the play often took a theological turn:

North Star. Let a cool breeze sweep in under my skirt and stroke me gently between the legs—it's like lying with God.

Galileo. What an immaculate conception!

*   *   *

All metaphysical considerations notwithstanding, however, as in most popular entertainments, the climax is what counts:

Galileo. (*Ecstatic*) Moan for me! Moan with the voice of the night setting in! Be the sunset herself, that great purple ass disappearing behind a veil of darkness!

North Star. (*Flickering with delight*) You have such a way with words, Galileo.

Galileo. Now be the moon! First flash me one white crescent, then a full moon, ripe and luscious!

North Star. Don't stop!

Galileo. I'll be the earth, and I'll send up a rocket.

North Star. How very modern!

Galileo. Countdown: 10-9-8-7-6-5-4 . . .

North Star. (*Starstruck*) Oh, oh!

Galileo. Now I'm a spaceship sailing for the moon, to dip my mast into your every crater, and land deep in your lunar lip . . .

Almost invariably, however, just when the play approached what promised to be a particularly gratifying finale, reality intruded in the form of a female shriek, of panic, not plea-sure—TOMMY!?

The intrusion occurred with such regularity that Krampf envisioned writing it into the script as the cry of the Inquisitor.

It was his mother calling from her room.

She wanted to know what he was doing.

Being an invalid confined to her bed, Mrs. Krampf was totally dependent on her son. He was her hands and feet and other atrophied organs.

YES, MOTHER! he replied immediately, dutiful son
that he was.
WHAT ARE YOU DOING, TOMMY? she inquired.
STARGAZING, MOMMY! he said.
THAT'S A GOOD BOY! she sighed relieved.

Once, long after midnight, his mother safely asleep and he
himself engrossed in nocturnal study of Milky Way II, his
telescope feverishly scouring the facade of the Hotel Beauregard, Krampf spotted a splendid asteroid several degrees
due north of the flickering red neon "B" of B E A U R E-
G A R D—a beauty to behold.
    With long red curly locks, full hips and pear-shaped
breasts, she hung out the window, feet dangling, her star-
studded kimono fluttering in the wind.
    Boldly she appeared to meet his gaze, the star of his
dreams.
    Shaken, stirred to action, Krampf freed the frenzied
needle of his compass, that jerked and rattled and faithfully
fastened on its mark, releasing the pent-up passion of the
aging, forty-seven-year-old adolescent that he was.
    For the next five nights he focused on her astral
charms, examining in turn her peaks and craters.
    And each night she returned his gaze, daring his lens
to go deeper.
    Moved to oratory, Krampf composed an ode that
began:

                    If I were a nose
                    I'd live in your clothes
                    I'd sleep where you slept
                    And creep where you crept . . .

and so on, concluding with the ardent wish:

> And you would crush me with your thighs
> And I'd delight in my demise
> To drown at sunset
> What a happy dream of death
> To wake in a stream of woman sweat
> In a cloud of woman breath.

Not bad, thought Krampf, and contemplated reciting it to her, or better yet, putting it to music and hiring a blind accordionist to accompany him as he serenaded her from beneath the tattered canopy of the Hotel Beauregard.

Thereafter, night after night, consumed by the onslaught of love, and unaccustomed to its hapless side effects, Krampf sat motionless at the window, awaiting her appearance.

But then, on the sixth night of looking, the window above the flickering "B" was barren.

And on the seventh night, its rickety frame was filled by the pitiful form of a haggard black transvestite massaging his breasts with motor oil, cooing endearments to the pigeons on the ledge—Here, pretty pretty! Here, sweet sweet!

Krampf cursed the night, and went so far as to imagine putting out his eyes, Oedipus-style; but imagination is one thing and painful reality quite another.

He returned to his puppets with redoubled intensity, but their wooden posturing failed to excite him.

He knocked their heads together in a fury.

In a mute stupor they lay there with cracks in their skulls.

*   *   *

And then one night the telephone rang, a thing it rarely did, since the Krampfs were very select about the company they kept and the outsiders they allowed to enter the sanctum of their trust, preferring solitude to the hazards of intimacy. Look at the mistake we made! his mother would often remind him. The *mistake* referred to her husband, his father, who, on a hunting trip shortly after young Krampf's third birthday, mistook his wife for a duck, and promptly flew the coop thereafter, leaving crippled mother and infant son to fend for themselves. Such is the price of intimacy.

Probably a wrong number, Krampf muttered, lumbering over to the telephone. Who is it!? he snorted, ready to hang up immediately if the caller asked for Carlos or fell into incomprehensible syllables of Newimmigrantese.

WHO IS IT?! his mother, awakened by the ringing, echoed and amplified his own annoyance.

A friend, replied a female voice in an unsettlingly familiar tone.

You must have the wrong number, Krampf grumbled, about to hang up.

Didn't you miss me? she asked.

Krampf faltered, at a loss for words.

I had quite a time finding your number, she continued, I missed our little game of hide and seek.

Is it *you*? he gasped.

Laughter on the line.

Where did you move to?

WHO IS IT, TOMMY!? his mother cried, WHO ARE YOU TALKING TO!?! she insisted with mounting intensity.

Who's *that*? the caller asked.

Mother, he said.

How sweet, said the caller, a mama's boy.

WHO IS IT!?!?!?!? the invalid shrieked.

Krampf cupped his hand over the mouthpiece. SOME-ONE DOING A SURVEY! he yelled, and removing his hand, whispered: When can I see you again?

When I feel like it, said the caller—click!

Hello! Hello! Krampf was frantic, confused, frightened and aroused, gripping the receiver then releasing his grip, afraid he might have strangled the connection.

WHAT DO THEY WANT TO KNOW!? his mother persisted at the same pitch and volume. FAMILY SECRETS? DON'T TELL THEM ANYTHING! TELL THEM YOU HAVE NO TIME! TELL THEM YOU DON'T GIVE OUT THAT KIND OF INFORMATION! . . . TOMMY!? . . . TOMMY?! she cried, TELL THEM TO LEAVE US ALONE!

I'LL TELL THEM, MOMMY, I'LL TELL THEM, he sighed.

When next the telephone rang some nights later, Krampf, who, having stretched the cord to its limit, could keep watch at the window all the while remaining within arm's length of the phone, was quick on the draw and caught it before the second ring.

Where are you? he pleaded.

Look! she replied.

A shade was slowly lifted in the window just below the luminous red "R" of B E A U R E G A R D—the surrounding "U" and "E" had long since ceased to function— a leg slithered out, pale and sultry, tracing circles in the neon glow.

Do you like it? said the voice.

Yes, he groaned.

That's all for now, regards to mother, she giggled and hung up.

Like a soldier huddled in his trench, not knowing whether to welcome or fear the future, Krampf dug in for the duration, however long it might last. Had he before derived a fleeting pleasure from his nightly peeping, it now had become an addiction, an obsession, a thing he could not do without, and on nights when the telescope offered no relief and the telephone failed to ring, Krampf crouched by the window and wept. Whereas his former life had at least offered the predictable satisfaction provided by his puppets, reality robbed him of such regularity, and shattered the tenuous order of his solo system, leaving the former puppet master a slave to the object of his desire.

To kill time, he traced a diagram on the wall and resorted to scientific speculation:

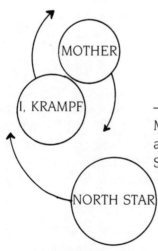

—Latched onto me, he mused, Mother is my MOON, but I too am *her* moon, as MOTHER and SON revolve around each other.

—Her lurid position in the SKY, *my* sky that covers me, at times like a blanket, at times like a veil, varies. She appears to be moving east, while I, Krampf, maintain a stationary position at the center of my system. But then it is altogether possible that she, in fact, remains still, while I keep moving elliptically around Mother, and that the two of us, Mother and Son, circle around *her*, so that when I do not see her, it is not that she has disappeared, but rather that I have my back turned to her.

Yet, on the other hand, if she *is* the North Star, whose light is the original source, hers or Mother's light (as there are no other celestial bodies of like magnitude in Krampf's universe), can it be that Mother is not my moon, but my sun, and Krampf is a mere planet blindly orbiting around her?

Or is the North Star not a star at all, but a parallel sun!

But then why did I never see her before!?

Or perhaps (and this was his most daring speculation), perhaps, mused Krampf in the course of his cosmological ruminations, perhaps I am the sun.

Meanwhile, there was Mother to contend with.

I'M TIRED, he complained when it came time for her Wednesday-night wheel around the apartment.

WHAT'S THE MATTER, TOMMY? she asked, immediately suspicious.

NOTHING, MOMMY, I'M JUST TIRED, THAT'S ALL.

YOU'VE ALWAYS WHEELED ME WEDNESDAY NIGHT! WEDNESDAY IS MY NIGHT TO BE WHEELED!

I'LL WHEEL YOU TOMORROW, he proposed.

WHAT'S WRONG WITH TODAY!?

I TOLD YOU, he said, losing patience, I'M TIRED, AND BESIDES, MY BACK ACHES.

SINCE WHEN?! she asked accusingly. SINCE WHEN DOES YOUR BACK ACHE!?

ALRIGHT, he conceded, realizing that any victory would be purely Pyrrhic, costing him more grief than it was worth. I'LL WHEEL YOU, he said, BUT ONLY FOR A LITTLE WHILE.

THAT'S A GOOD BOY! she said.

It was no trouble hoisting her out of bed and into her wheelchair, his mother didn't weigh much.

WHEN YOU WERE A LITTLE BOY, she beamed with pleasure, I USED TO WHEEL YOU ABOUT. DO YOU RE-MEMBER, TOMMY?

YES, MOMMY, he replied.

AND ALL THE LADIES IN THE NEIGHBORHOOD, THE JEALOUS SLUTS, WOULD LEAN OVER AND LOOK AT YOU. WHAT A LOVELY CHILD, MRS. KRAMPF, THEY SAID, WHY HE LOOKS JUST LIKE YOU.

YES, MOMMY, he said, YOU WERE LOVELY IN YOUR YOUTH.

AH YOUTH! she sighed. DID YOU REMEMBER TO WATER THE GERANIUMS?

YES, MOMMY, he lied. In fact he hadn't watered them in years, having long since replaced the real ones with plastic imitations.

YOU WHEEL ME SO WELL, his mother puckered her lips for a goodnight kiss, as he lifted her out of the chair and gently laid her back in bed.

Later, alone in his room, Krampf tried to imagine what making love must be like. Never having had any intimate physical contact with a woman before, his notion of the act was restricted to what he had read: What Lord Flimflam did with the chambermaid when Lady Flimflam was out galavanting with the gardner. Krampf practiced with his puppets. He drilled a hole in Judy's wooden pelvis suitable for the insertion of a finger.

Alas! cried Judy, the chambermaid, having been cornered in the parlor by the sly Lord Flimflam. Do not harm me, sir, for I am an innocent girl.

Lord Flimflam. My intentions are honorable, I assure you, my dear. For surely there is nothing more honorable than the mutual exchange of pleasure.

Chambermaid. Pleasure, Milord?

Lord Flimflam. Did your mother never teach you the facts of life?

Chambermaid. Never, sir!

Lord Flimflam. Then I will take it upon myself to educate you!

Chambermaid. Education is a wonderful thing.

Lord Flimflam. Come into my arms, my dear, and let me spell out the syllables of love.

Chambermaid. The word, I think, has but one syllable, sir.

Lord Flimflam. The act is multisyllabic.

Chambermaid. Shall I go fetch a pencil and paper for my lesson, sir?

Lord Flimflam. That won't be necessary. I'll be the pencil and you, my dear, will serve as the white page.

Chambermaid. How does a white page do, Milord? I'm afraid I'm quite illiterate.

Lord Flimflam. Paper is compliant.

Chambermaid. Like this, Milord? (*She lifts her skirt.*)

Lord Flimflam. That's it! And now, my precious page, prepare to take dictation!

Chambermaid. In longhand or short?

Lord Flimflam. Just open your pad and leave the penmanship to me!

The right forefinger poked about, found the hole and lunged, striking the complacent left palm. Wooden but willing, the chambermaid succumbed.

Days passed, days spent staring at the telephone, fondling the receiver, winding the rubbery curlicues of wire around his neck, lifting the receiver every few seconds, listening for the dial tone, then dropping it again, thinking: Maybe she's trying to get through to me.

Impatience prompted him to call up the operator.

There must be something wrong with my phone, he said. I never get any calls.

The operator checked the line. No, sir, she reported after the routine tests. There's nothing wrong with the equipment.

I tell you there's something wrong, he persisted. The phone never rings.

Maybe, mister, she suggested, your problem ain't mechanical.

A man accustomed to the mediation of windows has a hard time dealing with the immediacy of doors. For whereas the former filters out the disagreeable necessity of response, reducing life to the passive appreciation of a framed tableau, the latter demands participation, active involvement, the presence of body and mind. What the window holds at bay, the open door flings in your face.—

Knock knock
Who's there?
Ben
Ben who?
Ben looking for you . . .

It was Wednesday night, Mrs. Krampf's night to be wheeled, and she happened to be parked at the door when someone knocked.

I bring you salvation, said the voice that belonged to the knuckles.

Do come in, said Mrs. Krampf.

Salvation comes in various colors, the Bible-salesman, a young woman with thick glasses, red hair tied back tight and severe, an ankle-length black skirt, and Mother Hubbard shoes, expounded over the promise of milk and cookies in the living room. I personally prefer my Scripture sober black, she said, but there are those who go for celestial pink.

Pink? inquired Mrs. Krampf.

It depends upon your spiritual disposition, the Bible-salesman responded, I think it's nice to have a Bible for every occasion.

What a lovely idea, said Mrs. Krampf, pivoting her head (her only movable part) in search of her son—TOMMY!?—who, just then, chomping three chocolate chip cookies at once, clutching a boxful under his left arm and a pitcher of milk in his right hand, came stumbling in from the kitchen—DON'T STUFF YOUR MOUTH, FOR HEAVEN'S SAKE! she said, and pivoting back to her guest: I really

must apologize for Thomas's manners, we're not accustomed to company.

Blessed are the meek, the Bible-salesman smiled.

Hearing the visitor's voice, Krampf stopped dead in
his tracks and fixed his eyes on her.

We're offering a set of seven Bibles, a different color
for every day of the week.—The young woman proceeded
to unbuckle her briefcase and spread out her samples on
the glass-topped coffee table. Color, she explained, has a
profound influence on our feelings and actions, so why not
start each day off right!

Krampf squinted, trying to imagine the Bible-salesman
naked and bathed in a red neon glow. No, no, he concluded,
it couldn't be her!

Look! she said, pointing to the seven Bibles arranged in a
semicircle on the clear glass surface, such that they seemed
to be floating in the living room's densely domestic at-
mosphere.—Seven windows, seven tomes, seven temples
of color. You open yourself when you open the Bible, she
beamed a beatific smile. Pick a color, any color!

Green, said Mrs. Krampf, entranced like a child at a
magic show. I've always been partial to green, it's the color
of life.

Green it is, said the Bible-salesman, raising the
imitation-emerald-emblazoned cover. And to the back-
ground accompaniment of violins and harps, the Mormon
Tabernacle Choir sang:

To everything there is a season, and a
Time to every purpose under the heaven;

A time to be born, and a time to die;
A time to plant, and a time to pluck up . . . etc.

And while the music played, a mechanical rose attached to a green tinted wire stalk sprouted and wilted,
inspired and sucked back, so it seemed, into the very heart
of the text.—A timeless message every time! the Bible-
salesman insisted, Batteries not included.

How stirring, remarked Mrs. Krampf, who hadn't been
so moved in years.

Her son, of cynical bent and scientific temperament,
was less impressed. Deux ex machina! Cheap tricks! he
muttered, munching cookies.

YOU MIGHT AT LEAST HAVE THE COURTESY TO
THINK OF OUR GUEST! his mother chided him. GIVE THE
GIRL A COOKY!

Begrudgingly, grumbling all the while, Krampf plucked
an imperfect specimen out of the box, a cooky marred by
the craters left in the wake of dislodged chips, and lowered
it over the Bible-salesman's plate, when a wink, a surrep-
titious flutter caught him off-guard; the cooky missed its
mark and landed in her lap.

Excuse *us*, said Mrs. Krampf, scowling at her son. He's
a dear boy really, just a little clumsy, that's all.

Blessed are the pure in heart, for they shall see, the
Bible-salesman recited, and scooping up the wayward
wafer, allowed her hand to linger in the cleft of material
between her thighs. A second well-directed wink struck
Krampf like a blow to the solar plexus. Gasping, grasping
the pitcher of milk and the box of cookies as a drowning
man grasps after flotsam or a child the objects that conjure
up an illusion of security, he sank into the vinyl cushions

of the couch (the only piece of furniture large enough to hold him), his mouth a gaping circle of astonishment.

Tell me, said Mrs. Krampf (delighting, despite herself, in this rare spree of sociability), how did you come to such a fine appreciation of Scripture?

Daddy, God rest his pious soul, was a painter of religious subjects, and I was his favorite model.—The visitor nibbled kittenlike at the cooky's edge.—From Genesis to Revelations, I posed for every sacred scene.

Was he famous? the hostess inquired. Have I seen any of his works?

Oh yes, the young woman affirmed. They mass-marketed a deluxe 3-D version of Daddy's blinking Jesus. It's a very popular item on the mail order circuit, second only to brass facsimiles of Elvis Presley's last belt buckle.

How marvelous! said Mrs. Krampf.

And dare I forget, the Bible-salesman added, Daddy's colossal thirty-foot-long, multi-panelled Last Supper mural in the meat department of Alpha & Omega, the largest Christian supermarket in the country!

Like Leonardo da Vinci! the enraptured Mrs. Krampf proclaimed, hardly able to contain her glee, which, given that the rest of her was immobile, found its sole emotive outlet in a swiveling cranium and a flapping jaw. Imagine, she said, here we are entertaining the daughter of a famous artist, the model of immortal angels and saints! Your mother must be very proud!

The visitor's immaculate smile collapsed into a sullen glower.

I'm sorry, said Mrs. Krampf, perceiving that she'd touched a sensitive spot. Is mother deceased?

Oh no, the Bible-salesman shook her head: Mother disapproved.

Come again? said the hostess, arching her right brow in deference to her puzzled ears.

The Bible-salesman shrugged her shoulders: She didn't like the way Daddy looked at me.—

Mrs. Krampf inspected the face of her interlocutor, discovering, much to her dismay, a quivering lip and the alarming glow of sentiments best repressed.

The two women's looks interlocked like wrestlers squaring off in the ring.

Do have a glass of milk, it will calm you, *dear*, Mrs. Krampf prescribed. MILK, THOMAS! she said to her son.

Poor Krampf, present in body if not mind, flinched.

His mother's voice resounded in the echo chamber of his inner ear, striking the tympanum with a thundrous clamor, causing him a palpitation or two.

MILK! the maternal commandment rang out again.

And roused out of the catatonia that accompanies certain kinds of epiphany (the physical manifestation of which he did his best to camouflage with the fortuitous aid of the cooky box), Krampf rallied the reserves of his faltering self-control. Gaze glued to the twin globes partially eclipsed, though clearly evident in relief, rising beneath the black canopy of the Bible-salesman's blouse, he gripped the pitcher right manfully by the handle, tipped its spout over her chalice, and poured until milk swelled convexly in her hand.

My cup runneth over, she smiled at Krampf, and rounding the rim with her nimble tongue, skimmed off an inch of milk, and licked her lips.

*   *   *

Heavens! exclaimed Mrs. Krampf, struck by the sudden scandalous revelation that tongue and lips are flaps of naked flesh, in which case, talking is an unspeakable act, and listening equally corrupt. And what of looking? she reflected, concerned above all for her son's sake: Is not the eye the lewdest organ of them all!

Meanwhile, torn between filial devotion and the incompatible demands of desire, Krampf lost his grip and dropped the pitcher, which splattered and shattered at the Bible-salesman's feet.

Trembling with telescopic intensity, his glance lapped up the milk-soaked carpet, where shards of glass sparkled like stars in the soggy firmament.

If there is one thing an astronomer cannot long abide it is proximity. Put Outer Space between him and the object of his contemplation, and he is in seventh heaven. But place that heavenly body within arm's reach and all science fails him. He will burn up like a comet, and like the impetuous Icarus, his wings will melt like so much wax beneath the merciless gaze of the sun.

CLOSE YOUR EYES! his mother commanded. WE'VE SEEN QUITE ENOUGH!

Yes, Mommy, Krampf sighed, sinking back into the vinyl confines of a shrinking universe.

In silence, they continued to peer at each other: three planets, each set in its own orbit, each burdened by the force of its own unendurable gravity.

*   *   *

The Bible-salesman broke the silence.

You ain't seen nothing yet, she said, unbuttoning her blouse.

Stop Playing!

It was just past noon, when—I don't know if the violinist on the corner, the fact of his playing badly had something to do with it—the building broke its moorings and took flight.

You can imagine my annoyance, first, at being awakened—I like to sleep late—by the wretched whine of those strings, and second, after peering out the window, to discover that the distance between myself and the sidewalk below had more than doubled, and was fast on its way to tripling. I had always imagined that if things got really bad, I could leap the three flights down and end it all. But whereas a three-flight suicide is imaginable, a six-flight suicide is a dizzying and altogether disagreeable prospect, and nine flights—well, let's not talk about it.

Please, I cried, straining, under the circumstances, to maintain my customary politeness, will you stop playing! But already the violinist had become a mere speck of annoyance, and though, I repeat, I am not altogether certain that his music was to blame, I needed nevertheless to hold fast to some explanation, however irrational, for this strange state of affairs, and the suspicion that the violinist might be at fault was more comforting than that he might not.

Stop it! I cried, as his irritating strains dissolved into the anonymous agitation of the streets.

But the moment I lost sight and sound of him, he and his miserable music took on another, far more desperate form. They became an idea, an obsession, an anchor, indeed my only anchor to the world of the streets that now seemed all the sweeter to me the farther I floated from it. I shut my eyes tight and tried to force myself to see him and hear him again, to keep him alive in me like a little flame without which I would surely succumb to total darkness.

Stop playing! I howled out the window, but the earth and even the clouds have dropped out of view. I am floating ever upwards into an indigo sky with nothing but the fading recollection of a poorly played mazurka to remind me of how things were, and, I fervently believe, still are on the sidewalk below.

2. STINGS

The Sting
of the Real

"cette bouffée de réel"
—CB

—*Damn!* muttered Mr. Jones.

The boy leaned into the compartment, pointing to the seats across which the American had carelessly scattered his overnight bag, newspaper and raincoat before falling asleep. Just like Paramus, he had thought a peaceful moment ago, comforted by the familiar sight of the smokestacks, giant fingers of fire blazing in the orange twilight, giving in gladly to the rattle and sway of the train as it pulled out of Turin Central only to be roused by the sound of the sliding door.

—E *libero?*

Being the only passenger, he could hardly say no. But before he even had a chance to reply and gather his things, the boy had already hoisted his rope-tied cardboard valise up onto the luggage rack, plunked himself down in the facing window seat (from which Mr. Jones reluctantly removed his feet), pulled a rumpled Italian Western comic out of his back pants pocket, and as he flipped the pages, the man noticed with a shudder of revulsion that the boy had no thumbs.

Old fears surface suddenly: terror pickled in time.

Rufus Jones, of Elizabeth, New Jersey, a seasoned steel scrap salesman, unmarried, unattached, unmoved by anything but metal, was not as a rule given to undirected reverie. But the memory of a children's picture book read to him in the long distant past, its images etched into mind, disrupted his meditations on the slumping market for American steel and would not let go, try as he might to shake it.—I *beg you, son*! pleads the good-natured mother (eyes burning). *Stop sucking your thumbs*! Or *the tailor upstairs will surely come down one day and snip them off*! Oblivious as yet to the cruel fate that looms a mere five picture frames ahead, the rascal awaits his mother's departure only to resume his nasty habit, when the door flies open and in strides the terrible tailor, pale, haggard and fierce, white hair blowing in the wind of his awful purpose, eyes fastened on his mark, with his monstrous sheers unfurled . . .

—*Cioc-co-la-to*?

—H*uh*!? Mr. Jones bolted upright in his seat, startled by the unfamiliar voice and the green-eyed grin of the boy he'd forgotten was there.

—*You like*? The boy held out a half-melted bar of Nestlé's Crunch.

—*No thanks!* Mr. Jones shook his head, surprised and somewhat taken aback that the boy spoke English.

—*Bene!* The little fellow shrugged his shoulders and popped the sticky bar of chocolate into his mouth. Sucking and smacking his lips, he licked the brown smudges off his eight fingertips and two stumps. A proliferation of gold teeth glittered in the half moon of his grin and smile lines creased the edges of his green eyes.

Poor little fellow! the American thought, never having seen a child with wrinkles and so many gold teeth in his mouth. Feeling pity and regretting not to have accepted the boy's kind offer, he pulled out a box of Chiclets and rattled its contents out into his open palm.

—*Have a Chiclet!* he insisted.

The boy plucked up a little white square with the pincer grip of his fore- and middle finger and dropped it into his mouth.

—*Don't swallow, just chew!* the American said, demonstrating with his jaw, wagging a cautionary finger to his throat.

The boy laughed and proceeded to imitate him, aping his every gesture, from the puffy bellowslike inflation and collapse of his sagging cheeks to the out-of-sync ripple of his eyebrows, even doubling his childish chin, all of which Mr. Jones immediately recognized as a faithful, if less than flattering, replica of himself.

Embarrassed, annoyed, overcome by a sudden suffocating sense of proximity with his fellow passenger, he reached for the window handle.

—*How 'bout a breath of fresh air?*

—*No!* A fist came crashing down on his unsuspecting knuckles. E *pericoloso sporgersi!* . . . *Is dangerous lean out!* the boy shouted, pointing to a rusty metal plaque above the window with a warning in three languages to that effect.

Flustered and angry, uncertain of what to do now, whether to switch compartments or stand his ground, Mr. Jones resorted as he so often did in the face of confrontation to the safety of withdrawal; reaching for the newspaper on the seat beside him, he held it up above eye level.

KOREAN JETLINER MISSING NEAR SOVIET PACIFIC ISLAND

The headline hit with a rush of horror and relief, a cozy illicit comfort in distant tragedy. "A South Korean airliner disappeared this morning near the island of Sakhalin," he read on. "All 240 passengers and 29 crew members are believed . . ."

—*Bang bang, you dead*!

Mr. Jones lowered the paper. The boy had his forefingers pointed at him, *Gunsmoke*-style. There was nothing to do but laugh. This little display was so obviously an attempt to make up.

—*Handsome pair of six-shooters you got there, son*! the American joked, prepared to forgive and forget.

—I *Carlo the Kid*! the boy said, blowing on the barrels of his improvised pistols.

—*Rufus Jones, glad to meet you*! the man replied, heartily shaking the extended hand, a little stunned at the strength of its grip.

—*You Texan*? the little desperado inquired.

—*New Jersey*! The salesman shook his head. The boy looked disappointed. *Not everyone*, said Mr. Jones, *can be a Lone Ranger*.

Carlo cracked a smile.

—I *Texan*! he nodded.

—*Is that a fact*! said the man, his eyebrow raised in doubt.

—*Houston Test pilot, Ace Number One*! the boy beamed, doing a thumbs-up with the stump of his right hand.

—*You don't say*! said Mr. Jones. *You know*, he added, *I wanted to fly myself when I was your age. Never did earn my wings though, guess I just didn't have the right stuff, huh kid*! he winked.

The boy returned a blank uncomprehending look.

—*But you can't always live with your head in the clouds*! the man insisted, pointing from the top of his head to the night sky that hung dark and low outside the window of the speeding train.

The boy still registered no response.

Detecting a hint of adolescent scorn, and feeling a growing annoyance at the boy's apparent inability or unwillingness to comprehend, the man found himself raising his voice:

—*Why waste your life on the wild blue yonder*!? *Embrace reality, for heaven's sake*!

The boy mimicked his agitated eyebrows.

Embarrassed at his uncharacteristic outburst, yet all the more adamant in his desire to pursuade, Mr. Jones lowered his voice, resorting to the empassioned whisper he generally reserved for important pitches, big big deals.

—*You don't understand me now, son, but you will someday*! he said. *I traded hollow pipe dreams for the tangibility of metal scrap*! *It's a living, a good one too*! *Makes you plenty of this*! he said, digging into his pocket and pulling out a handful of change.

The boy nodded and grinned.

—*You see what I'm saying now, don't you*! the salesman smiled triumphantly.

—*Look*! the boy said, and with consummate sleight of

hand plucked a coin out from behind Mr. Jones's right ear. *Feel!* he said, and before the man realized what was happening, the boy was rubbing his thumb against the sharp edge of the coin, a five lire piece shaved down razor sharp. D*is lucky coin!* the boy assured him, *It save you life sometime!*

The man pulled back his hand. Bewildered he stared at the boy whose face looked a little older than it had a few moments ago, the smile lines more pronounced, the gold teeth glittering all the more brightly.

—*You know you'd make one heck of a salesman, son, if you put your mind to it!* the man said, licking the wounded ball of his thumb. The train whistle shrieked, perhaps to warn an imprudent vehicle of its approach. Accidents do happen, the American reflected, remembering reading of a crash near Calais where a daredevil boy on a motorcycle had failed to clear the way in time.

—*Attenzione!* the boy crouched down low. He cast a cautious glance first at the window and then at the door, then pulled down the shade on both and brought his lips up close to the American's ear. CIA *Specialista aquatica!* he confided in a security-conscious whisper, displaying an ID card that looked like it had been torn off the top of a box of cereal. KGB *catch me . . . I take coin . . . swish . . . like dis!* he demonstrated, passing his hand quickly across Mr. Jones's throat, grazing the skin ever so slightly.

—*Just like James Bond!?* Mr. Jones laughed nervously.

—*Non mi credi?* Anger furrowed the boy's forehead with an adult intensity, his voice dropping a decibel in pitch. I *show you prove!* And leaping up out of his seat, he dragged his suitcase down off the luggage rack, tore open the cord, bent back the cardboard lid, and pulled out a loaded speargun, pointing it at the American's throat. *Carlo the Kid mean business, you bet!* he said.

Mr. Jones felt the tickle of the cold metal tip. His heart beat in time to the rhythm of the train. Thumpety-thump . . . thumpety-thump . . . thumpety-thump. Hands flat at his sides, back shoved up against the sticky leather of the seat, feet hard against the floor, he pressed his tongue against the tasteless wad of gum lodged up against his palate to keep from swallowing.

—*Bang bang!* the boy laughed.

The American opened his eyes to find his fellow passenger peering at him with a look of concern. The cardboard case had been replaced overhead—no speargun in sight. His tie had been loosened, his collar button opened, his shoes removed. The boy was fanning him with the comic.

—*Okay, Mister?* he inquired. *You wan' a Coca Cola?*

Just out of Florence, the compartment door slid open and in stepped the conductor.

—*Biglietti, per favore!*

Better tell him, decided Mr. Jones. The boy is dangerous, he has a loaded weapon in his luggage and is quite possibly psychotic. But something kept him from opening his mouth. The conductor more than likely spoke no English, and what good were his two or three words of Italian? Nothing had happened, nothing really. Nothing but the antics of a troubled child whose eyes touched him now with a green intensity. What was there to tell after all?

—*Biglietti!* the conductor repeated impatiently.

Mr. Jones reached for his raincoat, dug into his inside breast pocket where he always kept his travel documents. Funny, he thought, finding it empty. He rummaged through the remaining pockets, relieved at last to find the ticket folder.

—*Here*! he said, handing it to the conductor.

The conductor carefully examined the folder, shook his head and handed it back. His humorless look spoke for itself.

The folder was empty.

Agitated now, the American turned his raincoat upside down and proceeded to shake it. A few toothpicks and an empty box of Chiclets fell to the floor.

The conductor scowled and turned to the boy, who calmly reached into the pockets of his pants, pulled a wrinkled train ticket out of one, while from the other, Mr. Jones noticed, the blue tip of a U.S. passport peaked forth.

—*Hold it*! he shouted, shaking all over as the conductor reached for the ticket.

The conductor paused, looked from the man to the boy and back to the man.

—*Can't you see*!? Mr. Jones cried, pointing at the hand that held the ticket. *Can't you see? . . . he has no thumbs*! (It was not what he had meant to say, but these were the words that slipped out.)

Cursing in unrestrained Italian, annoyed at such an unseemly disruption of ritual, the conductor shook his head, took the ticket from the boy, punched two holes in it and handed it back.

—*Allora, Signore*! he said, turning to the stunned Mr. Jones, who stared back in silence.

The boy pulled out a wallet.

—*Io pago per lui*!

It was then that the salesman felt the absence of the familiar bulge in the right front pocket of his pants and thrusting his hand in, found nothing but a five lire piece.

The conductor spit out another string of expletives,

took the money from the boy, punched the requisite two (plus three supplemental) holes in an orange penalty ticket which he tore off his official pad and tossed disdainfully at the American's feet.

—*Porca Madonna!* he muttered, violently sliding the door shut behind him.

Mr. Jones followed the receding sound of his footsteps in the corridor till it mingled with the rattle of the train.

The boy popped a Chiclet into his mouth and smiled.

Run! said the voice of reason.

But something other than reason had taken hold.

In every game of cat and mouse there is a moment, however tenuous, when the cat turns his back, out of carelessness or calculated cunning, inviting the mouse to attempt escape. This is a crucial point in the game, a climactic interlude. The mouse may make a run for it, or throw itself at the mercy of its whiskered opponent. Logic, in any case, accords with the instinct for survival; clemency is unlikely. But weary of the game, hypnotized into submission perhaps, the mouse more often than not awaits its fate. A moment of madness or ultimate lucidity? Does the mouse hope against hope? Or is it quite simply enthralled by the claws of the cat?

—*You like E-Mickey E-Mouse?* said his fellow passenger, pulling out another comic.

As the train rolled into Rome's Stazione Termini, Rufus was humming the hundredth refrain of the Mickey Mouse Club Song:

> M-I-C—*See ya real soon!*
> K-E-Y—*Why? Because we like you!*
> M-O-U-S-E . . .

—*Aspetta qui!* said the man, handing Rufus a rope-tied cardboard suitcase, picking up his overnight bag and raincoat. I *be right back!*

Rufus nodded.

It was all he could do to keep from raising his thumb to his trembling lips. Mustn't do that, he remembered, rubbing the thumb against the sharp edge of the coin in his pocket, feeling, like a distant reminder, the sting of the real.

Sid and Darling

Darling collected interesting people. She liked to boast to her friends—those of the ordinary kind—that she knew "the weirdest people in the world."

For instance, she had befriended a man with no bottom half, a man who moved by propelling himself along on a skateboard.

She'd first seen him in the park, Washington Square: a normal, even handsome and muscular torso sticking up out of the sidewalk as though he'd been buried waist-deep while the cement was still wet, and so had become a kind of living statue.

His name was Sid—or that's what the park crowd called him—as he came whizzing by on his skateboard the day he ran into her. Quite literally. Well, it wasn't really he who ran into her, but sort of the other way around. Darling stepped into his path, apologized profusely when Sid toppled off his board, and tried to help him back on—but his strong manly hands shoved hers aside as he lifted himself back onto the little chariot.—"You wanna watch where you're goin', lady!"

"I'm sorry! I'm terribly sorry!" she said. "Are you alright?"

"I'm okay!" he snorted and pushed on, his powerful hands paddling down the pathway.

Sid wore a black beret and he had a bullet for an earring. He had long black hair, a short beard and dark flashing eyes. Darling found him very handsome indeed.

The next time they met, which was about a week later, Sid himself rolled up to her as she sat on a bench, pretending to be absorbed in *The Ladies Home Journal.*

"Nice day," he said.

"Yes, it is," she agreed, looking up in surprise—"Oh!" she exclaimed, meaning: Oh, it's *you!*

Sid had a knack for filling in the missing words. He could hear what people didn't say. "Yeah, it's me!" he said, "You stepped in my way on purpose the other day, didn't you!"

"I don't know what you're talking about!" she said. He made her a little nervous now. His tone sounded just a little too intimate.

"Listen, lady—I may look like half a man, but I'm all there, if you know what I mean!" he winked.

"Oh!" she said.

"What's a matter, you deaf and dumb or somethin'? Don't you understand English?"

"Well I don't usually make it a practice of getting intimate with strangers."

"Well we're not strangers anymore—are we!" he grinned, reaching up and rubbing her stockinged knee. "My name's Sid, what's yours?"

"Darling," she gulped, feeling the pressure of his strong hand on her thigh.

"Darling, that's a funny name."

"I like my name!" she protested.

"Listen, Darling, honey," he said, "Wada ya say we take us a little walk together?"

"You don't waste any time, do you?"

"Come on!" he said, once again placing his hand on her knee, only this time reaching up a ways under her skirt to where the stocking meets the garter clip, and he snapped the elastic against her skin.

He led, she followed.

Wordlessly they moved in a procession-like silence.

"Heh, Sid!" yelled one of the roller skaters in the park, "Save some for me!"

Darling felt both thrilled and shamed as the passersby, trying not to look, turned around at the last minute to stare, wondering: What's *she* doing with *him*?

"Come on!" he commanded, slapping her ankles, "In here!"

He led her down a ramp, through an alleyway, back into a sheltered truck loading zone not visible from the street. And before Darling could take stock of the situation, a hand crept up her leg and unsnapped the garter.

"Wait," she said, "I don't really know you!"

"You will!" he whispered, sliding the stocking down her shivering leg, rolling himself up under her with the confidence of a skilled mechanic.

She felt the cold metal of the bullet earring slide against the inside of her thigh. "Why do you wear that?" she asked.

"Nam, baby!" he muttered, already otherwise occupied with his tongue—"That's the shell that didn't get the other half of me."

Our Lord of
Washington Square

That summer they descended on the Square.—

A hoard of long-haired saints, gospel pushers with their fatuous smiles, peddling Love with a capital L, they mingled with the multitude to save strayed souls.

And the multitude for the most part was amused.

Even the Rastafarians nodded, shook their dreadlocks and smiled the benign smile of enlightened tolerance, one devotee to another.

The mood, to use a favorite catchword of the 70s, was mellow.

Tightrope walkers, fire eaters, glass dancers and guitarists of all styles competed for the crowd's attentions— any moment a show might break out—while frisbees whizzed by overhead and scateboards cut incredible pirouettes an inch away from your ankles.

The Rastas kept everyone well supplied—Loose joints 'n bahgs, Mahn, got that gold weed, check it aout! And the newcomers tried for a piece of the action:

Put Christ in your life!
Put this up yours!

It was not the first influx of out-of-town prophets to try their luck in Washington Square Park.

Every year, the Menonites make the long trek in from Lancaster, PA, to New York City by chartered bus, arrange themselves in choral formation (somber-faced bearded basses to the rear, their primly bonneted soprano spouses up front, with the alto offspring huddled in between) and serenade the minions of Babylon with Anabaptist fervor.

Carmelites and Tibetan monks, Franciscans, Cistertians, Hare Krishnites and Chassidim have all made forays into the park.

What is it that attracts them to this squared-off oasis of anything goes? The chance to cast their spiritual nets in a bona fide sea of iniquity? To have it out with the devil on his own ground? Or is it the subliminal lure of the bones? For beneath the pavement lies an old potter's field lined with anonymous earthly remains, and where the fountain now gushes a gallows stood in former times, until the prospering gentry who built their red brick townhouses around the rim of the field, objected to the sight and smell, and the nasty business of hanging was moved uptown a ways to Union Square.

July dissolved in carefree reverie. The locals stretched out on the lawn, puffing Jamaican splif, meditating on the vastness of the universe and the moves of sinuous females engaged in Oriental exercise. August came, as always, ac-

companied by a blast of heat, Manhattan heat, the kind
you stick in like chunks of fruit in cherry Jell-O.

The blond missionary should have known better than to
wade out into the middle of the fountain in sparse attire,
her shorts hugging tight, her tee shirt soaked and see-
through, with a bible in one hand a pair of New Testament
sandals in the other.

Heads turned slowly, lizardlike; eyes followed with distant interest and a few catcalls rang out; still nothing much
else would have happened, considering the degree of heat,
had she not suddenly decided to kneel down in the filthy
water, lift up her hands toward the muggy heavens and
declare at the top of her lungs: I AM JESUS CHRIST COME
TO BRING YOU THE MESSAGE OF LOVE!

True, revelation strikes when and where it will, and who is
to say lower Manhattan is any less ripe to epiphany than
Fatima or Lourdes!

The girl stood up, now dripping wet. She climbed atop
the water spout that formed a perfect little round stage,
posed Venus-on-the-halfshell-like, with water spewing
forth dramatically around her, shouting: LOVE ME FOR I
AM THE LORD!

You bet, baby! replied a stoned biker, a self-designated
spokesman for the crowd that now, roused by the promise
of a show, pressed closer 'round the fountain, hooting and
cheering, the general consensus being that Christ could
not have picked a better body to return in.

THE SPIRIT OF THE LORD IS UPON ME, this Jersey
Joan of Arc cried out: HE HATH SENT ME TO HEAL THE
BROKENHEARTED . . .

The catcalls swelled in pitch and intensity, along with a noisy puckering of lips.—Heal me, baby! the biker crooned.

Meanwhile, the perplexed apostles stood by with mixed emotions.—Susan, come out of there! a concerned sister called back. But a brother restrained her.—Hold it, sister, he said, stroking his scruffy beard, The Lord works in wondrous ways!—Praise the Lord! they all echoed in harmonious unison, reaching out to embrace the as yet unredeemed bystanding sinners, who, conditioned to the subtle touch of pickpockets, spun 'round in a rage: Lay off!

WATCH AND PRAY THAT YE ENTER NOT INTO TEMPTATION, the girl in the water spout sang out, encouraged by all the attention. THE SPIRIT IS WILLING, BUT THE FLESH IS WEAK, she warned, her ample bosom heaving. AND I SAY UNTO YOU, ASK AND IT SHALL BE GIVEN, SEEK AND YE SHALL FIND, KNOCK AND IT SHALL BE OPENED UNTO YOU . . .

Take it off! the biker yelled.

TAKE IT OFF! the crowd took up the call.

No doubt innocently wanting to prove a point, the girl shook her head and smiled a luminous smile: THERE IS NOTHING COVERED THAT SHALL NOT BE REVEALED, NEITHER HID THAT SHALL NOT BE KNOWN, she preached and proceeded to peal off her tee shirt.

TAKE IT OFF! TAKE IT OFF! the crown went wild, their collective libido stirred to a fever pitch.

The biker could control himself no longer. He tore off his own tee shirt, tossing it as a tribute of sorts into the fountain, whereupon a host of like-minded Samaritans did the same. Displaying a magnificent grinning devil's head tattooed across his wide back and snakes slinking down his hairy arms, the biker leaped howling into the pool, and waded out toward its center, catching the baptismal spray in his face, flapping his arms like a hungry sea lion about to pounce on a fish.

Already he had his hands wrapped 'round the prophetess's bare middle and had hoisted her into the air when a well-aimed nightstick caught him squarely in the small of the back and sent him reeling into the fetid drink.

Did someone call the Romans, or were they on hand all the while, plainclothed and eager, watching with the multitude, waiting for the kiss of Judas?

There are those who claim to have seen the girl walk away calmly across the surface of floating tee shirts. Believe what you like! Strain at a gnat, and swallow a camel, as the scripture says. August, in any case, is a bad month for miracles.

It's Hard
to Be a Fish

"It's hard to be a Jew!" Rabbi Fein, our Hebrew School teacher told us with a trembling intensity and the sickly smile of a martyr. We boys agreed and wanted no part of the whole unhappy business.

To our wild eleven-year-old eyes, the Hebrew letters he scrawled in white chalk on the blackboard were a nagging reminder of all those THOU-SHALT-NOTs. In each letter we saw the bony white fingers of the dead wagging and waving, whispering NO! to all that we desired. And every day we boys betrayed the dead. We extended the spindly legs of the holy letters into crosses and swastikas, fired spitballs 'round the room, and dreamed of the freckled girls of Our Lady of Fatima, with their pigtails, bobby socks, short plaid skirts and their pale white Catholic school skin.

"Now boys!" Rabbi Fein clapped his hands to try to attract our attention. "Who remembers about Noah and the flood?" He waited patiently. We stared out the window and yawned. Oh how we pitied and despised that sad scarecrow of a man with his shabby blue suit and pious enthusiasm! We sneered at every word that spilled out of his thin spinstress lips. "Noo!?" said the Rabbi, grinning—"Who remembers?" And he opened his bible and read aloud: " 'And the Lord, Blessed be He, regretted that He had made man on earth.' "

"What about women?" Fat Freddy inquired. We giggled and grunted, elbowing each other in the ribs.

The Rabbi turned red. "W . . . w . . . women too!" he stammered, wiped his sweaty palms on his pants and continued: " 'But Noah found favor with the Lord. For Noah was a *righteous* man.' " He paused—"I don't suppose any of you little scholars knows what a righteous man is!?"

"A real schtuper!" Carl called out, thrusting his right fist forward under his left. We snickered, pretending to understand more than we did.

"Sha! Shtill!" the Rabbi yelled, waving a limp forefinger. Carl sneered contemptuously. He was the tallest, toughest kid in the class, having been left back twice and already approaching his barmitzvah. He boasted of his exploits with the Marys and Eileens, and once he pulled out a packet of Trojans as proof—though none of us knew what they were for, and thought when he unravelled one, that they must surely be the cut-off finger tips of his mother's rubber kitchen gloves.

"A righteous man," the Rabbi raised his voice, trying to command respect, "is a man who finds favor in the eyes of God."

"Rabbi! Rabbi!" Fat Freddy waved his chubby paw.

"Yes, Ephraim?" the Rabbi smiled hopefully.

"Is it true for a fact that some men find favor in the eyes of God?" Freddy asked with a convincing sincerity.

"Indeed they do!" the Rabbi nodded.

"That means," Freddy reasoned, "God must be a faggot!"

The whole class howled in delirious laughter. Rabbi Fein summoned up the last shreds of his authority: "That will be all, Ephraim!" He pointed to the door.

Freddy marched out cheerfully with a mischievous swagger, and we knew that we were in for some fun.

As soon as the waves of laughter subsided, the Rabbi perused our ranks for a flicker of interest. His gaze alighted on little Herbie, the only one of us who ever did his homework (his mother was president of the temple sisterhood). "Tell us, Hillel"—the Rabbi's voice quivered, aching for an answer—"why did the Lord, blessed be He, open up the floodgates to destroy mankind?"

Herbie rose to respond. "Because the Lord, blessed be He . . . ," Herbie began in a pious whisper, and would have dutifully rattled off the rest had not Carl just then swiped Herbie's brand-new fountain pen and squeezed out its contents all over Herbie's clean white shirt. Herbie turned to grab for the pen. Carl skillfully tripped him and sent poor Herbie sprawling to the floor.

And then a great miracle happened.

It started with a trickle and soon swelled to a steady stream. Water was rushing in under the door. A rusty, bubbly, foul-smelling rivulet.

We climbed up onto our desktops, squealing with delight, tore pages out of our notebooks, and floated paper arks down the aisles. Carl had little Herbie pinned face down with his foot, and in burst Fat Freddy, wheeling a mop and pail.

"It's a flood, Rabbi!" Freddy announced, trying hard to hold back the laughter—"The toilet won't stop!"

Rabbi Fein rose slowly out of his chair. His lips trembled, strange unintelligible syllables issued forth and a darkness fell over his face. "Animals!" he cried out with a biblical rage, long simmering, that had now all of a sudden boiled over.—"For dust thou art, and unto dust shalt thou return!" And then he lunged for Freddy, grabbed him by his collar, lifted him effortlessly into the air, carried the fat little boy, too stunned to resist, to an open window and threw him out.

We gaped in awe and wonder.

Meanwhile Carl was giving Herbie compulsory swimming lessons. Little Herbie gasped and gurgled. Carl tried to console him—"It's hard to be a fish!" he said.

Carolina Street

Mrs. Parry was a bitch. Nobody on Carolina Street would have denied this, least of all Cindy Schwartz, teenage daughter of her next-door neighbor, whose fiancé Morty Mrs. Parry stole for her own use.

Mrs. Parry had blond hair and a beauty that reminded of polished porcelain. She was a favorite of the canasta crowd who sneered as she wiggled past their porch, walking her little white poodle.

We never saw much of Mr. Parry, who worked three jobs: pharmacist, teacher, and weekend door-to-door vacuum cleaner salesman—to support his wife's habits; she collected shoes and men.

Once her daughter Dolly showed me her mother's summer shoe collection. There were at least a hundred pairs of high heels, pumps, slippers and sandals—and this, Dolly reminded me, half-proud half-ashamed, was just a fraction of her year-round supply.

*   *   *

One day Mrs. Parry was out walking her poodle and stopped in front of our porch. Now despite the fact that we all considered her a bitch, she was an aristocrat of sorts to our summer colony and demanded special attention. Mr. Kamen, the grocer, who cheated you on your change when you bought your bagels (and whose son is now a respected congressman from the district) always served her first. Her porcelain smile promised certain possibilities, though I was too young to understand what they were. Still something about Mrs. Parry made me nervous. So when she stopped in front of our porch to let her poodle sniff a particularly savory heap of white dried droppings, I did what I had long since fallen out of the habit of doing: I went in my pants—number two: THE BIG ONE!

A small crowd of street regulars including fat Julie and Sandy the brat started smelling it. But I was glued to the spot, terrified that if I moved, someone might notice the lump in my pants. Everyone presumed, much to Mrs. Parry's embarrassment (who went around drenched in colognes and perfumes) that her poodle needed a bath. She beat the dog mercilessly. She mistreated anyone close to her who had the audacity to embarrass her. Once she had tied her son up naked to a telephone pole because he had refused to go to bed early when Morty came by.

It was a summer of the awakening of strange nameless sensations.

I came to a few basic conclusions about life. That some people, namely Julie, the girl upstairs, were fat because they were sad, though they smiled all the time to hide it. Julie was an adopted child.

And then there were the people who made you slightly sick, the way you get on a long car ride, like Frances, the ageless mustached daughter of the Zimmermans, who sat day after day in her black dress on her parents' front porch, greeting us as we passed on our way to the beach. And I realized that it was her destiny to sit out her life on her parents' front porch.

And another thing I realized.

It was after Dolly had been teasing me and I chased her along the beach, caught her finally by the bottom of her black two-piece, and innocently, unintentionally yanked it down, baring what the Coppertone ads advertise.

I stopped dead in the sand. Dolly stared at me and I stared back. A new realm opened that afternoon and it was stronger and stranger than anything I'd ever known.

That summer the Drifters made an AM hit out of "Under the Boardwalk," and pretty blond Laura dived from the high board, having forgotten to take out her bobby pins; one entered her ear; the doctors said she would be paralyzed for life.

And she was the prettiest girl on the block.

The Gate

I used to swing on a white gate. Not a big one or a fancy one, just a simple little wooden contraption that swung so smoothly on its hinges. I'd hug the boards and kick off with my right foot and the gate went flying shut. Then I'd lift the latch and the pendulum of my seven-year-old fury flung it open again. Back and forth I swung, oblivious to time, at peace with the ebb and flow of life as I'll likely never be again.

Now I was always trying to devise a means of attaching myself to the gate so that I wouldn't have to hold on, to let my head dangle, hands hanging free, and come ever closer to the ecstasy of total abandon. With washing line and terry cloth cord I tied myself to the white wooden slats, but after ten swings or so, my bindings invariably came loose and I landed with a thump on the hard cement.

The solution came to me by accident, as most solutions do. In my frustration after one fall too many, I kicked the fence and got the tip of my sneaker caught in between the slats. And I thought, if I could get a sneaker caught by accident, then I could surely do it on purpose. And if it worked with a sneaker, then why not with my knee? I shoved and squeezed and managed finally to get my left knee lodged in place.

Pleasure knows no clock. I was an eagle and the hours melted toward noon.

"Martylein, lunchtime!" my mother chirped from the shadow of our bungalow doorway. I cursed. I fumed. I pretended not to hear. Then the rusty squeak of our screen door insisted: "Komm schon, Kind!—it's getting cold!" There was no refusing her now. The thrill of it all had worn thin anyway. The sun was pounding, my left knee ached and hunger devoured my fervor.

I pulled but the knee wouldn't come out. I jerked it and twisted it but that poor knee was swollen red and refused to budge. "Martin!" she called.

I tried, I really tried to make it come loose. I knew she'd be getting anxious and I certainly did not want to get caught in such a ridiculous position.

My knee pulsed painfully. My heart beat out the seconds.

Mother sent my brother out to see what was keeping me.

He delivered his report loud enough for the whole block to hear: "Marty's stuck in the gate!"

Mama came running. "Um Gottes Willen!" she cried.

Something like this had happened to me once before on the beach when an angry clam chomped down on my inquisitive thumb and wouldn't let go till Mama brought a rock to smash it open and all I wanted was to see what was inside.

Word spread down Carolina Street and before long the whole community was alerted to the enigma of a boy attached to a gate. The curious flocked by to witness the spectacle and to offer remedies: Coppertone, a sledge hammer, a hacksaw, a baseball bat. I kicked and punched at anyone who came near.

Finally our next-door neighbor, Arnold's father, the doctor, knocked out my knee with a surgical reflex hammer.

Tears burst the dam of my little boy's pride and drowned any shreds of the morning's long-gone thrill. I never swung on the gate again. It would be years until I felt even an inkling of such ecstasy, under cool sheets in the dark, my knees intertwined with others, thrusting and bellowing like a bull.

The Story of
the Ball and the Wall

This is the story of the ball and the wall. I have often tried to tell it, but it always got stuck in my throat as if it just didn't want to be put into words and would rather remain untold. I'll give it another try.

I was walking past a wall, not a wall really, but a high wooden fence. I had often passed that wall before without taking any special notice. There are plenty of walls in the city. But this time I heard children's voices on the other side. Must be a school, I thought, or a private playground. Nice, isn't it, that such places still exist where a child can play, peaceful and protected. I wouldn't have thought anything more about it, would've walked on by, and that damn wall would not have turned into a dark disturbing memory, if something hadn't just then flown over it, hit me on the head, bounced off dully, and rolling into the street, revealed itself as a somewhat underinflated soccer ball. I bent down and picked it up.

Now this wall, which was in fact a fence, was made of

high vertical wooden slats set at a slant, so that if you approached it from the direction from which I came, it looked absolutely solid. Imagine my surprise then when out of this seemingly solid wall a hand stretched forth. Later I realized, of course, that there were narrow spaces between the slats, but at that moment it was as though the wall had grown a hand, a trembling little child's hand.

Followed by whimpering.

The wall was crying.

Fearfully and a little perplexed, I stepped closer. And then I saw a pair of eyes peering out from between two slats.

I held the ball up in the air and was about to toss it back over the wall, but the whimpering grew louder.

Don't you want your ball back? I asked with my eyes.

Then a second hand poked through the slats and together the two waved at me, insistently.

What do you want!? I said with my shoulders and hands. The strange thing was that I, who am normally so talkative, had neither the desire nor the inclination to open my mouth. It was as in a dream where the all-meaning gestures suffice.

The hands kept on waving, beckoning me closer, and I followed until no more than a few inches still separated those frantic fingers from my cheek.

And then I saw the other children, and the attendants in their white coats. Children playing alone, because they are not quite conscious of the presence of others. Special children, as we are wont to call them nowadays.

And here was one such special case who saw and recognized the bars of his cage as such.

Two hands reached through the wall. They weren't reaching for the lost soccer ball, that was only a pretext.

No, they were reaching for me. To touch me, to feel a body from the other side, with longing and affection and something akin to love.

Did I feel compassion? No.

A shiver of revulsion went through me—I couldn't help it. I tossed the ball back over the wall, and seconds later, as I rushed off, reminding myself that I was already late for an appointment—maybe I was, I don't remember—I heard the dull thump of rubber hitting the pavement.

The game was about to be repeated.

Wet Pain

Marny and Rosemarie rode between the subway cars for kicks. That's what you do when you're fourteen and feeling the first rosebuds of sex appear, counting the hairs and killing time.

Look't me, Marny yelled, doing a handstand, gripping the rims of both cars as they ground together and rounded the bend.

Hot shit, Rosemarie commented coolly, leaning against the open sliding door, sucking the last life out of a dying roach. Her tits were already swelling and the older boys approved. I just seen a rat the size of Nelly's melons, I swear, she shouted over the roar of the train.

Marny came down with a thump, planting her sneakers squarely where her hands had been. Gimme a hit! she demanded. It's dead, said Rosemarie, nicking the still smoking fleck of paper down onto the tracks. You suck, Marny hissed, feeling a bottomless rage building inside. She stared at the bulges in Rosemarie's tee shirt and comparing them to her own puny bee stings, wanted to shove the bitch in the path of the shrieking metal wheels, but Rosemarie was her best friend and it'd be hard to find another. Marny didn't make friends easy.

No sweat, honey, Rosemarie laughed, I got more where that come from. She pulled a long, thin, tightly rolled joint out of her hip pocket, applied her lighter and took a couple of very short ladylike puffs.

    Gimme that, Marny grabbed for it and stuffed it in between her lips. Marny inhaled deep and long, like there was a hole that needed to get filled.

What's a matter, honey, you got pussyache? Rosemarie asked, cool as ever.

    Yeah, said Marny, faking a knowledgeable swagger, nothing that a good nine inches couldn't take care of. Rosemarie laughed. My cousin Ernest, she said, you should see it, I swear—I'll loan it to you, okay!? Okay!

    They passed the joint a couple of times back and forth until they were both good and happy. Meanwhile the screech of steel on steel was getting too intense for their tender ears and the little ladies stepped inside.

It was the long limbo hour after midnight when the 9-to-5ers are all holed up for the night and the wildcats are out on the prowl. The subway car was empty of other riders.

*   *   *

Hoodjoo like better, Marlboro Man or Camel Man? Rosemarie raised the question, studying the cigarette ad over the doorway they'd just passed through. The door kept banging open and shut.

Camel Man's a pussy, Marny sneered.

Yeah, Rosemarie agreed, jumping up on sudden inspiration and applying her lighter to the posterior of a smiling Senor Enrique Vargas, an unfortunate hemorrhoid sufferer. He could use a little fire up his ass, she prescribed.

The two girls giggled and tore through the car, setting fire to battered children, asthmatics, victims of the common cold, a bright-eyed young black doctor grinning on behalf of the American Negro College Fund and a very realistic plate of chicken and rice—Yum yum! Rosemarie licked her lips.

Then they ran to the next car over and sat down, gasping and panting from all the laughter, smoke and fun.

Rosemarie was all tired out, but Marny hadn't had enough. She was starting to come down and that always made her cranky. I'm beat, Rosemarie sighed.

Shut up, Marny snapped back, her wild eyes scanning the car for some new source of amusement. Look, she cried out overjoyed, pointing to the far end of the car where in a heap of newspaper a man lay stretched out asleep. Come on, Marny commanded, and Rosemarie followed dutifully, loyal best friend that she was.

His face was all shriveled and shrunken like a balloon the morning after a party. Pink patches showed under his thinning hair. His lips were blue. His pants hung loose. In his arms he cradled a half empty bottle of Poor Irish Rose.

He stinks, Rosemarie said, holding her nose and turning away.

Hold it, Marny stopped her, I got an idea. She reached over and slowly, carefully tied his open shoelaces together, peering all the while into his open zipper. I don't think he has much use for it anymore, do you, she said, slipping the bottle out from under the man's arms.

Rosemarie shook her head, a strange smile of comprehension and complicity curling 'round the edge of her lips.

Marny worked fast.

She uncorked the bottle and poured its contents all around inside the rusty metal of the broken zipper.

His eyes blinked awake as the cool wetness ran down his legs. He grinned uncomprehending at the two girls who leaned over him.

Gimme the lighter, quick! Marny yelled and Rosemarie handed it to her mechanically, her eyes fastened in a trance, as the little flame shot out like the tongue of a snake.

At first the man realized only the loss of his bottle, and spotting it in Marny's hands he lunged for it and missed. Only then did he notice the flames, see them first, then feel them, for alcohol dulls the senses and delays the perception of pain. And reaching in between his legs, he let out a terrible howl. He tried to rise, but his tied laces only further confounded his befuddled attempts and he landed squirming and screaming on the floor.

Later, standing alone on the station platform, the next to last on the line, not far from where they lived, the two girls were still giggling. The car doors slid shut. The airbrakes sighed. They listened a while longer until the rumble of the disappearing train swallowed up all other sounds.

Rosemarie pulled out another joint. Gimme fire, she said. Marny rummaged around in her pockets. Shit, she said, I must 'a left it on the train.

Dumb cunt, Rosemarie chided her affectionately, hugging her close.

Billy's Story

That day, the one I'm talking about, all the kids crowded around me. Look't Billy, they said, he's dressed up like a girl.

I'd taken my sister's dress, put it on and gone for a walk.

I don't know why I did it. Just 'cause I felt like it, I guess. That's the first time I ever let her out, Mary, I mean— my other me.

She's a mean bitch, that one. Won't let me sleep at night when it's her time.

Anyways, I found out real quick that I'd better keep her shut up inside. Boys don't do things like that, my mother said. But I do, I said, or I mean, Mary does. Who's Mary? she wanted to know. Mary's me if I wasn't me, I said. And she laughed because she was used to my saying and doing funny things. They were funny to her, not to me.

I was a funny kid in other ways too. I didn't like baseball

or stickball or ringolevio or those sort of games. What I liked best was to climb on top of the garage and hide out. I didn't do anything much up there. Just sat and stared mostly. And wondered about things.

About where Gramma went when they said she went to Florida but I knew she didn't because how come we couldn't ever go visit her down there?

Another thing I liked to do was stand in front of the hallway mirror and look into the other place, where another boy whose name wasn't Billy except that he looked a lot like me and I played Simon Sez.

Simon Sez stick out your tongue!

I did it and he did it too.

Simon Sez pull down your pants!

We both looked around to make sure nobody was watching.

Simon Sez make your snake grow!

And then it did that funny thing that it does, his and mine. It stretched and stiffened up. And I felt that funny feeling that I felt when I watched Carol across the alley undressing in front of her open window and she hadn't pulled the shade and didn't know or care that I was there watching. Then he and I both of us ran to the bathroom when it happened.

Shut up, Mary! I'm telling a story.—Yeah, you're in it too!

I don't know what Billy's been telling you about me—(that's me, Mary talking now)—but I'm really a very good little girl. I never lift up my dress for boys to look at. Never, except for one time when Billy wanted me to.

*   *   *

Mary, you'd better shut up!

Go on, lift up your dress, he said. We were alone up on the garage roof—he'd stolen his sister's dress again. Go on, he said. I'll take my snake out of my pocket and show it to you. It was a hot day so I didn't mind. I just waved my dress in front and his snake got stiff and hard, and then it did that thing that it does. And he got my dress all wet and I couldn't take it back then, could I!

Shut up!

I'll tell you another thing I did once.—(It's Billy back)—I always used to wonder about my sister's talking doll. The one where when you pull a string it says: Hi, I'm Talking Tina. And when you pull again, it says: Do you want to be my friend? Well I just wanted to find out where the words came from.

So I took a kitchen knife and cut her up. I found the place.

It was a little round box with holes in it.

Girls don't have a snake so I guess they gotta have something.

Hotdog Is Dead

My muse, said Rosamund, is my pink and purple puppy. Originally mutt-gray, the puppy endured the mood swings of its mistress, a hairdresser of decidedly quirky bent. To each new color change lathered into its pelt, the puppy replied with a feeble whimper.—You look gorgeous! Rosamund insisted.

Most of the time the dog sat quietly in a corner of the hair salon Rosamund ran on East 7th Street.

What's its name? clients asked.

I haven't decided yet, said Rosamund, shears in hand, gleefully snipping.

Going to get your hair cut by her was like—well, picture the Delphic Oracle with scissors! You might come out bleached blond or with islets of tuft bobbing in a sea of pinkish scalp. It all depended on Rosamund's mood. Sometimes she'd even turn away a prospective customer—I don't feel anything from you today!—which gave her an air of exclusivity.

One heavy metal rocker arrived with black bristles streaming helter skelter and emerged with a Telly Savalas. Changed my life, said the rocker, Rosamund brought out the latent Buddhist in me.

Others had less conciliatory things to say.

The chic's a real Delilah! shrieked the drummer and lead vocalist of The Dogs, weeping in the wake of the Sherman's March of her scissors.

The moon tells me to chop, she said, and I chop.

Andy Warhol dropped by once.

Is it true blonds have more fun? Rosamund asked.

Andy reflected. I guess so, he said.

Rosamund handed him a mirror, and without so much as snipping a single strand, said: How do you like it?

Perfect, said Andy.

When the Dalai Lama dropped by for a trim unaccompanied by his usual cortege of attendants and followers, Rosamund recognized him immediately from his picture in *Life*. Please, she said, handing him her clippers, holding forth her own head.

Celebrity has its price though.

The moment Rosamund began to feel freeze-dried inside, as she put it, she sold the salon and skipped town.

In Upstate New York, she knocked on the gate and sought entry to the cloister of Our Lady of Cairo, but had second thoughts when the Mother Superior refused her puppy. We don't admit pets, she said.

Rosamund wandered.

Sometimes by bus, sometimes by plane, sometimes by chauffeur-driven limo.

In Shreveport, Louisiana, she finally decided to give the dog a name. How about Hotdog? she said. He replied, as usual, with a complaisant whimper.

On a bus from Louisville to Nashville, Hotdog suddenly expired.

With the creature in her arms and tears in her eyes, Rosamund scoured the Country Music Capitol in search of a neon sign maker, and when she found one, explained: I want you to make me a fifty foot tall pink and purple flashing neon sign that says: HOTDOG IS DEAD. The sign maker looked puzzled. Don't worry, Rosamund reassured him, opening her purse, pulling out a handfull of hundred dollar bills. I don't believe in credit, she said.

Motorists and truckers were stunned by the mammoth neon announcement that sprouted one day in the vacant lot between Taco Rico and McDonald's, a message attached to no fast food concession, advertising nothing but itself.

It's an eyesore, McDonald's complained.

It's Un-American, a vice president of public relations at Taco Rico who had worked his way up from teenage taco stuffer charged.

Sorry fellas, said the State Commissioner of Public Space, Long as she pays she stays.

Rosamund bought herself a Chevy pick-up, the back of which she had outfitted as a camper, and drove it up and down the highway admiring her sign.

At sundown she rolled up under it.

I like it here, she decided, squinting up at the pink and purple flashing memorial. Listening for the familiar whimper, she fell asleep in the grid of intersecting headlights, dreaming beneath a neon moon.

Miss Marcy

Marcy dreams of ships. Great big freighters, ocean liners, frigates, barges, schooners and sloops. Anything big enough to carry her far away from her miserable fourth-floor walk-up existence.

The steps creak and sag beneath her monumental weight as she climbs and descends. The neighbors' doors are always open and she hears them not even bothering to couch their comments in a decent whisper: There goes the whale with her mutt!

It is true. Marcy is a sad and giant woman whose only joy is the affection she can shower on the little Chihuahua that she carries around in her purse and her dreams of sailing away.

—How're you today, Miss Marcy? How's the pooch?

These are ritual questions that require only a ritual nod. It's the children that ask the real questions:

—How come you're so fat, Miss Marcy? How'd you ever get to be that way?

Marcy smiles a fat woman's smile. A smile full of tears and daggers. Her breathing is heavy and she has to concentrate on each step and hold tight to the rickety banister, and watch our for rotten boards that the landlord refuses to fix because he'd like to get all the renters out and sell the land to a developer for big money.

Arriving at her destination, the downstairs front door or the door to her apartment, is always an achievement to be celebrated by sitting down.

Marcy sits down.

One day, she says to the Chihuahua, one day we are going to take a big trip. Wouldn't that be nice?

The Chihuahua barks several highpitched barks that merit a biscuit.

Good girl, says Marcy, stuffing the cookie into the animal's mouth.

Slowly then she rises from her sedentary position, and in the case of a descent, hazards the six remaining steps down to the street. The front steps are made of stone, at least they don't creak.

She likes to imagine the pavement all flooded as it once was many years ago during a childhood hurricane. On that day the rain transformed Carolina Street into the Grand Canal. She spotted a door torn off its hinges serving as a raft to the neighbor's boy (now long since married and gone), and called to him in that long-ago memory. Take me with you, Jimmy! she cried. You gotta be kidding, laughed the frecklefaced boy, you'd sink me for sure, you fat tub! And she cried, and ached inside every time that memory ripped through the skin of the present.

It is difficult for her to fit through most doorways, and

she isn't quick enough to tackle the treacherous electric sliding doors at the supermarket. She has to go in the back way, the delivery entrance, where there are two doors that can both be opened at the same time.

Mostly she has her groceries delivered, and the real destination of these perambulations is the beach, a mere five blocks away but a good hour's trek, considering her condition.

Sometimes she takes the dog out of the bag and lets it run beside her on a leash.

That's a good girl, she says, patting her and stuffing another biscuit into her mouth once the dog has done its business and can once again be dropped back into the bag.

Marcy always feels happy the moment she rounds a certain corner and gets her first whiff of sea air. Of course, she can't walk in the sand. A bench on the boardwalk will do. There she sits with her back to the land, scouring the horizon for any passing vessel.

Marcy dreams.

One day they'll take me with them. And she imagines herself on the deck of the Queen Elizabeth, walking her dog. How do you do, Ma'am, the captain says, his accent ever so slightly Skandinavian. Fine, she says, beaming. What's his name? The captain inquires. It's a she, captain, Marcy blushes. Of course, he says, how foolish of me.

And the vessel sails and sails, never reaching any destination.

After a while, the Chihuahua starts barking and Marcy realizes that it is time to go.

Wearily, sadly wakened from the sweetest of dreams, she rises from the bench, taking one last long look at the water before heading back home.

Arthur Fried

Arthur Fried, a lonely and rather overweight proponent of animal rights, arrived at the "Love Your Dog Day" Convention with high hopes.

He'd tried Weight Watchers, Alcoholics Anonymous (even though he never touched a drop of anything stronger than Coca Cola); he'd even replied to a personals ad, enclosing a photo of himself taken ten years ago at an amusement park in which he is holding a rifle and aiming it at the moving metal ducks—he hit no ducks, nor did his letter elicit a single response.

But today he hoped to change all that.

The desk clerk handed him his key, and he obediently followed the snooty porter who had in the meantime grabbed his bags and shuffled toward the elevator in front of which he planted them and held out his hand.

"Couldn't you take them up?" Arthur asked timidly.

"Not on your life!" the porter said. "I don't know what the hell you got in them bags, but they weigh a ton and besides, the elevator ain't working."

Arthur looked up and to his pained dismay, there was an OUT OF ORDER sign tacked to the elevator door. "When are they going to fix it?" Arthur asked.

"Tomorrow maybe," the porter said, begrudgingly pocketed the fifty cents that Arthur held out and stormed off cursing below his breath.

Three flights of winding hotel stairs are no joke—especially if you happen to be lugging two heavy bags filled with the necessities of life.

Arthur never went anywhere without taking his portable TV (he didn't trust any others to work right for his exercise program in the morning); a tape recorder because he fancied himself something of a writer and liked to dictate his thoughts to the machine in hopes of someday publishing them—of course, devoting all (or at least a considerable portion of the proceeds) to the cause of animal rights. The bag also contained his own pillow and sheets, a hair dryer—he never went out with wet hair, terrified as he was of catching pneumonia; a set of weights, allegedly portable; a chest stretching gizmo; and a week-long supply of lima beans and brown rice. Arthur was very particular about what he ate.

*   *   *

Suffice it to say that he eventually reached his room, and that the light didn't work and the water never got hot, but things were otherwise acceptable.

He lay down on the bed, stared up at the ceiling and thought about dogs.

The truth is, Arthur didn't like dogs, couldn't stand them in fact ever since at age six the neighbor's dachshund sunk its teeth into his leg.

Back downstairs in the big hall an old woman approached him.

"Are you one of us?" she asked, looking him over from head to toe and somehow suspecting that he might be one of the many fur industry undercover agents that the movement is convinced the industry plants to sow discord in their ranks.

"Oh yes," Arthur assured her, pulling out his SAVE THE PUPPIES button and pinning it onto his lapel.

"Well then you'd better hurry up and get inside, the meeting's about to begin!"

"Thank you," Arthur smiled, not quite knowing what he was thanking her for, information or absolution, and rushed into the auditorium. What amazed him was that among all the animal lovers there wasn't a single pet dog present.

"I wonder how come nobody brought their pets," he whispered into the ear of the aging Miss beside whom he decided to plunk himself.

The woman scowled: "We have no pets!"

"I'm awfully sorry," Arthur said.

*   *   *

The meeting had only just begun and already Arthur was nervous. And then he felt the sudden call of nature.

"Excuse me," he said to the aging Miss, climbed over her and ran out of the room.

"Where is it!?" he pleaded with the porter, the same one who'd refused to help him with his bags.

"Where's what?" the porter replied impatiently.

"The Little Boy's Room," Arthur whispered.

"JOHN'S DOWN THE HALL AND MAKE A LEFT!" the porter yelled back.

Arthur felt deeply embarrassed. "But that means I have to walk right through the meeting!" he said.

"That or hike upstairs," the porter suggested.

"Oh I don't think I could make it upstairs," Arthur confided.

"In that case," said the porter, "it don't look like you have much of a choice, do you!"

Now Arthur slunk back into the meeting. Someone was chanting: "ANIMAL RIGHTS NOW!" from the stage, and the crowd echoed his call.

Arthur tried to melt into the wall.

Then the old woman who hadn't much liked his looks before spotted him slinking sneakily along. "UNDERCOVER AGENT!" she called out to the crowd, and in an instant all eyes were upon him.

"MINK MURDERER!" the crowd howled, casting the red and burning beam of their rage upon him.

Poor Arthur Fried, he couldn't control himself.

*   *   *

And later he had to hike up the three flights of stairs carrying his shame in the seat of his pants.

He didn't meet any girls on that trip either.

Of Bread and Words

There is a small but well-stocked supermarket in my neighborhood; situated just opposite the gates of a major university, it attracts two distinct clienteles. Those who patronize its premises, replete with gourmet delicacies and overpriced staples, tend to be associated with the university: students, professors and administrators, they do their shopping here, oblivious to the prices, because of the market's convenient location, and for the most part, tend to be white. Outside meanwhile, attracted by the lure of plenty, panhandlers congregate within a radius of three feet from the electric exit door. The latter group, by and large black, banks on the conscience and goodwill of the former. But the real color difference here is green.

I live three blocks away, and am a regular customer.

I will on occasion drop a quarter in passing into the wilted paper cup extended at me. Sometimes I give cheerfully, sometimes out of superstition (to forestall bad luck or hasten good fortune), sometimes begrudgingly, but more often than not the bags weigh heavy in my hands, and I'm in a bad mood and can't be bothered.

The response, in any case, when I do give, is generally as uninspired and automatic as the act of giving. My counterpart's ritually muttered "Go' bless you!" followed by my own equally programmatic "Ta' care!" I may recognize a man because I have seen him around, but any acknowledgment of such recognition on his part or mine is purely perfunctory, a matter of habit as opposed to courtesy. For, in fact, we do not really see each other. He to me and I to him remain indistinct features of the urban landscape: a human mailbox and a faceless mailman—the traffic light is more alive, at least it changes color.

For some time now I have been aware of the haphazard presence of an odd couple outside the market. The younger man is white, bedraggled, and virtually incoherent. The older man, in his mid-thirties (about my age), is black, neatly attired, and very much on top of the situation. They work the pavement together, alternating requests, and sharing the spoils.

One evening not long ago, I was feeling in an open frame of mind.

The disheveled white beggar pounced on me as I emerged from the market. "Gimme money!" he pressed me, his manner not threatening (because he was so clearly out of it), but definitely disagreeable.

"Don't crowd him out!" said the black man, who moved up behind him, and gently eased him aside. "Leave the man his space!" he commanded, and acknowledged my discomfiture with a savvy twinkle and a sympathetic smile.

I smiled back, and dropped quarters into both men's cups, and while the younger man moved away, grumbling indecipherable curses at the sidewalk cracks, his companion shook his head with the solicitude of an older brother.

I cannot remember how we got to talking, or the exact words of the conversation that followed, but its substance has stayed with me.

We moved back several feet beyond the periphery of the panhandling zone, and in so doing, stepped out of the strict confines of quotidian time and space, shedding the differences that would ordinarily have defined the conditions of our interaction.

"I'm a baker, when I can find work," he said, flexing the leathery palm of his right hand, reviving it from the stiff round mold of the paper cup. "Man, I know how to knead that dough," he demonstrated in thin air, "it's like loving—you got to have the touch!" he grinned, winking at a woman walking by.

"I'm a writer," I responded, proudly displaying the callus on my right middle finger.

"Say, tell me the truth, ain't it boring putting all them words on paper?" he inquired, one craftsman to another.

"What dough is to you," I explained, "words are to me."

"I hear you," he nodded, "Gimme skin!"—and when I paused an instant before extending my hand: "Come on, man, you ain't gonna leave a good hand hangin'!"

Our palms met in a slap, we were speaking the same language, standing on a tenuous drawbridge spanned between separate worlds.

He beamed and I beamed back.

"I'm gonna tell you something I never told nobody," he said, "and I don't know why I'm telling it to you."

And what he proceeded to tell me is an account of

the last time he participated in a mugging. He was thirteen and running with an angry crowd. The leader was a brawny older boy who liked to push his weight around. They lay in wait in the bushes of a local park, and jumped the first white boy stupid enough to wander by. And the big boy yelled: "You better give us your money!" And echoing the war cry, *he* yelled: "Yeah, white boy, you better give us your money!" Only afterwards, when it was all over with, and they had a lousy five spot to split between them, for all the hurt and humiliation (he could never put enough hate into his punches), he felt as if *he* had been robbed of something worth more than a slip of green paper. And on the way home he jumped the big boy, heavier than him and twice his size—"It wasn't never like me to hurt nobody, but I punched all the pain out of me."

Whites, he told me, were all faceless and rich, made to be mugged—until he got drafted, and found himself bunking down beside a boy from Kalamazoo, "as white as a Hostess Snowball." It was the sixties, and the two of them did everything together: chased women, smoked dope, dropped acid, and he remembers staring at the grass on the ground on one trip, thinking every blade is the one and only. "I watched 'em and heard 'em growing, couldn't take a step less I crush a life."

And I told him about when I was twelve and bicycling with a friend round the edge of the black ghetto near where I grew up. We were on our way to an amusement park, and stopped to help a black kid lying under a bike. Only it turned out to be a trap, and five others dodged out from behind parked cars. I opened my mouth, about to say: You can have my money ($3.50 in nickels and dimes), now let's talk!—which is how I'd always imagined I'd react if I ever got mugged—but a hard right to my solar plexus was all the punctuation I needed to know that words were useless here, and the knife held to my throat dispelled my last illusions of eloquence. All I knew as I stood there was liquid fear. I was still trembling when a bus stopped in the midst of traffic, and out jumped the big black driver swinging a baseball bat, and scattered my faceless attackers; still trembling when a patrol car rolled up later to see what was holding up traffic, and the officers yelled: "What the hell are you doing *here!*" And had it not been for the black man at the wheel of the bus, the scars of fear would have taken far longer to heal, the panic that overcame me for years every time I saw a group of black teenagers gathered on a streetcorner.

And here we were, standing face to face, man to man, exchanging painful memories.

A writer, a baker, a candlestick maker—it takes all kinds to populate a city.

I wondered aloud what he was doing on the street, if he knew how to bake.

He had worked a while at a donut joint, he said, "but that ain't quality." He hinted at a problem with alcohol, said when it got to him he had to hit the street.

I said I understood the ache that makes you thirsty.

Politely then, excusing himself, he mentioned it was time to get back to business.

The white panhandler was rudely accosting customers.

He shook his head: "That boy don't know nothin' about bread!"

Corned Beef Hash

"Try talking to a man," Doris suggests (fishing for stray socks in the dryer), "with who what he's saying is in the future, but what he's really talking about is in the past—figure that one out, will ya!?"

Jill looks up from her folding, almost in tears: "Christ," she says, "I lost the collar button—Hank'll kill me!—off his best shirt!"

"Are you listening?!" Doris demands.

"I'm listening, I'm listening!" Jill assures her.

"So I'm standing at the register ringing up groceries, see—"

"Peanut butter still on special, Doh?"

"Nah, that was last week! This week's corned beef hash"—(Doris works at the A&P, has been ever since her husband Petey got laid off at Bullova Watch. Jill's Hank drives a hearse for O'Fearon's Funeral Parlor, and won't let her get a job, so she depends on Doris for all the important news:)—"Two for a dollar, Anne Page, only personally I wouldn't feed it to my dog!"

"I thought Petey liked Anne Page!"

"I said I wouldn't feed it to my dog—my husband's another story!"

"You're bad," Jill snickers.

"I know," Doris grins. "So I'm standing there, waiting on a regular customer, Old Man Harper, you know, the one that likes baked beans? I says to him, I says: 'How's the Missus?'"

"You didn't!" says Jill, "I told you Hank carted her off last Friday."

"I forgot," says Doris, who doesn't like being criticized or interrupted. "So anyways, he says, 'My wife, my Eloise, God rest, gave up the ghost last Wednesday.' 'Gee, I'm awful sorry,' I says, 'the beans are on me—'"

"You're all heart, Doh!"

"Get off it," Doris replies with a backhand swipe at the air. "What do you think he does then? Calls me an angel of mercy and kisses my hand."

"They're like that, the bereaved," Jill asserts on good authority, "very demonstrative."

"'Go home, Mr. Harper,' I says," says Doris, "'Go water your geraniums!'"

"Lord love him!" Jill sighs.

"Where was I? Oh yeah," Doris continues. "So then this tall skinny fella I never seen in the market before wheels a cart full of corned beef hash up to my counter and starts stacking it in little piles of two."

"He must like the stuff, I guess," Jill suggests.

"That's what I says to him, I says, 'I guess you must like it alright, hunh?' He don't say nothin'. 'The hash,' I says louder, thinking maybe he don't hear so good, 'you must be partial to corned beef hash!'"

"Hank don't eat nothin' canned," Jill confessed, lovingly folding a shirtsleeve, "he's a very particular eater."

"You wanna know what that man said to me, or don't you!?" Doris glares. " 'The boys will be hungry,' he goes—the way he talked, I swear, he sounded just like Vincent Price!"

"You know that bamboo steamer they're always advertising late night on Channel Nine?" Jill interjects.

"Yeah—!?" Doris fumes, dying to get on with her story.

"Well I finally went 'n sent away for it about a month ago, and day before yesterday morning it arrives C.O.D. I figure I'm gonna surprise Hank when he gets home. He says, 'What's that?' I says, 'It's steamed chicken, honey, just like on TV!' He says, 'Well I don't like the way it looks—' "

"So listen!"

"I'm listening!"

"So I says to him, 'You sure must have a lot o' kids, Mister!' 'N he looks at me with them red eyes like, I dunno, like he was Dracula's cousin or somethin'. He goes: 'The boys will be hungry!' "

"This lady out in Ronkonkoma had sextuplets, all boys," Jill advises, "and all on account of Vitamin C!"

Doris is adamant: "So I ring it all up and bag it, see, and he hands me this address to deliver—"

"Did you?"

"Did I what!?"

"Did you deliver the corned beef hash to the man?"

"We delivered it alright. The manager says for Bobby to bring it over. Bobby takes the bike out at half past four, it's five, it's six, it's a quarter after and he ain't back yet—"

"He have a accident?"

"Listen, at half past Bobby comes in shaking all over.— 'Bobby,' I says, 'where you been?' I know Bobby, he don't waste no time like them other boys. Took him a whole ten minutes to calm down, then he told us—"

"What?"

"The address."

"Was it a bad neighborhood?"

"Bad neighborhood nothing, it was O'Fearon's Funeral Parlor!"

"Practical joke, hunh?"

"Some joke, listen! This fella that was in here, he musta gone straight over there after. He says to O'Fearon, he says: 'I want you to get five caskets ready and fill 'em with plenty of food. The boys will be hungry,'—just like that, only nobody don't pull the wool over an undertaker's eyes. So then Bobby brings by the delivery and O'Fearon puts two and two together and calls up the station house. They follow that man home, find him in the backyard on his hands and knees clawing the dirt like a dog digging for a bone. The police identified the bodies of five boys, Bobby says he knew two of 'em from little league practice. The man taught Sunday School in Elmhurst!"

Jill is jubilant: "There it is!" she cries out, spotting a little white disk at the bottom of the empty dryer.

"That man taught Sunday School in Elmhurst, can you believe it!?" Doris repeats, incredulous.

"Yeah, I mean no," says Jill. "You got a needle 'n thread?"

"What for?" says Doris.

"The button," she says, "I'd better sew it on good, Hank's gonna have a lotta drivin' to do."

"You're hopeless!" says Doris.

The Milkman
Isn't Coming Anymore

The milkman isn't coming anymore. Housewives hereabouts are very upset since they now have to carry the heavy bottles themselves. The story is on everyone's lips.

Our former milkman, Mr. Hahn, was a bachelor and still lived with his old mother in the same house in which he was born and raised. His father had been a milkman too, and after old man Hahn kicked the bucket, young Hahn took over the family business.

Early mornings, long before the sun flashed her red cheeks, if you happened to stir out of a deep sleep, you might hear footsteps outside, the gentle tinkle of glass against glass and the murmur of a truck engine. But no one ever thought of burglars. It's only Hahn, you told yourself, turned over and went right back to sleep. And later at breakfast you poured out glassfulls of the fresh cold drink, and grownups and children alike licked it up like greedy cats.

Nobody knew the milkman personally. Sure, they'd

pass him in town from time to time, his gaunt, lanky figure always dressed in white. He'd nod, never say a word, and was known as a loner. But private life is private life, and so long as you behave in a decent, law-abiding manner, nobody pokes his nose into other people's business around here.

Well one winter morning there was no milk outside. You asked next door, but the neighbors hadn't had any milk delivered either. And the next morning, no milk again. And so a long milkless week went by, until a cat led us to the root of the mystery.

Miss Gottesman, chairlady of the local chapter of the Society for the Prevention of Cruelty to Animals, noticed a scrawny little kitten scratching and whining at the back door of a house on the outskirts of town. Poor thing! she said to herself, and pounded energetically on the door. A child is crying! that fine upstanding woman complained. But seeing as all her preaching and pounding came to naught, she turned the knob and pushed the door open— it wasn't locked, she said. The cat ran in and Miss Gottesman followed, to have a few serious words with the parents of that poor abandoned child. Deeply distraught, she later reported:

I saw empty and half-empty bottles lying everywhere about. And in one corner of the dark kitchen, in a tub filled with milk sat Mr. Hahn. He was pouring milk over his head and gargling with it; he laughed out loud and I shivered in my shoes.

Good morning, Miss Gottesman! he said—just like that.

For God's sake, Mr. Hahn! I said, and wanted to turn

around and run for it, but fear kept me glued to the spot.

Then he spoke to me very quietly, like there was nothing wrong.

A glass of milk, Miss Gottesman? he said, and took a glass down from the cabinet over the tub, dipped it into his bath and held out a glassfull.

My mother died today—he said, without the least trace of sadness. And then all of a sudden he laughed again like before, stood up, climbed stark naked out of the tub and started dancing 'round the darkened room. Milk dripped from his hair and hands.

The cat licked the drops off the floor . . .

Photograph of a Kiss

He was a strange little man, Sasha Gleb was, wandering the streets of Paris all day long with his camera ready, in search of the perfect picture.

"You're a fool, Gleb," his friend, the writer Isaac Babel, had told him years ago. "The only perfect thing in life is death!"

"This is true, Isaac Emilevich," Gleb conceded, "but a man is born with certain passions which he may not ignore.—You, for instance, would sooner die than misplace a comma or a period"—Babel smiled—"and I, well when I was a boy they wanted me to wear glasses. 'Sasha,' they said, 'your vision is blurry!' 'No,' I said, 'the universe is out of focus!' "

In 1917 Gleb offered up his camera to serve the people.

His photographs appeared on posters and in magazines. One poster in particular, later the subject of controversy (whose caption, composed by the poet Mayakovsky, read: THE PEOPLE'S DREAM) showed peasants at work in a field. Critics quick to recognize "Brueghel's epic sweep," praised Gleb for his "positive revolutionary outlook." Then one influential columnist, whose opinions stirred action in higher circles, noticed a detail heretofore overlooked. In the upper right-hand corner of the photograph, half-hidden by the tall grass, a young peasant girl with her skirts hiked up is crouching, presumably to relieve herself. The columnist charged Gleb with a "cynical disrespect for the brave daughters of the Revolution." The posters came down that night, and a week later, still reeling from the sting of the people's sudden disfavor, and fearing the inevitable fatal repercussions, Gleb fled to Paris.

The city suggested a limitless array of subjects. Elegant ladies strutting down the grand boulevards, gentlemen in hot pursuit, salesgirls smiling hopefully out of shop windows, gargoyles spitting rainwater, sinuous hands clutching long brown loaves of bread, barges carrying cargo and destinies down the Seine, clochards curled up asleep beneath the bridges—Paris seemed forever posing for her picture, and Gleb was glad to oblige.

Yet every time he aimed, focused and shot, the photographer's heart plummeted from expectation to despair: again he had missed it (if only by a fraction of a second), that elusive coincidence of light and shadow in which the observant eye can glimpse eternity.

Sasha Gleb was not one to give up. In his darkroom at night (a sealed-off corner of his kitchen), Gleb patiently incubated his visions, fussing over each negative, studying and judging the faults of each print as it emerged from the developing fluid, most of which found their way directly to the dustbin. Sometimes a print would be spared and left lying around the kitchen, among old cheese and dry bread.

"What's this?" a friend over for coffee would ask.

To which Gleb would invariably reply: "Trash!—Take it if you like!" Friends and visitors were never sure if Gleb really meant what he said, and some suspected that these few prints had been planted by a sympathetic hand to be saved from the judgment of a merciless eye.

When asked why he refused to exhibit recent work— his last exhibition at the Gallerie des Beaux Arts had elicited an enthusiastic response from critics and collectors alike, but that was in 1922, and ten years had since elapsed—Gleb shrugged his shoulders: "I have nothing to show!"

Still every day without fail he took to the streets.

Like a hungry leopard, a photographer stalks his prey. He must slip into a kind of invisibility, camouflaged by passing trucks and kiosks, invisible even to himself, and in a certain sense, cease to be, or rather become seeing, so that when a subject suggests itself, crystalizing suddenly out of the random flow of life, his eye can lunge and pounce and dig its teeth into the throat of the moment.

Today for some reason Gleb's trigger finger was nervous.

He had snapped a roll of pictures of a boy and a girl

playing hide 'n seek in the Parc Monceau, until their mother or nursemaid noticed him and suspecting some illicit intent on the part of the strange little man with the camera, came charging at him with her parasol and nearly smashed his lens. Gleb escaped, regretting only that he had failed to record that instant when suspicion flared up into rage and rage so stirred that otherwise placid, rather plain-faced matron, transforming her for a tenth of a second into a mythic Fury.

His finger twitched uncontrollably.

He stopped at a café for a glass of wine. Though it wasn't normally his custom to drink while shooting, he thought that perhaps the wine would calm his agitated finger.

It was then that Sasha Gleb took the picture for which he is so justifiably famous.

A couple passed close to his table, a man and a woman.

His hair was disheveled. She was not particularly pretty.

There was nothing really striking about either one of them except that they happened to be passing at that very moment, two figures in the crowd, preceded by a man in a trenchcoat (whose face is cut off in the photograph), and followed by a man wearing spectacles and a beret.

Without thinking, Gleb reached for his camera, just as the man turned, tipped back the woman, whom he held in his right arm, and it was as if Gleb's finger dislodged itself from his hand and soared across the incalculable distance that separates one life from another, dissolving, as he bent down to her, as her right hand (the visible one) went limp, and forces of the universe converged in a kiss.

Waiting for
the Mailman

There is no sweeter, more painfully pleasurable pastime I know than waiting for the mailman.

Over years of attentive listening in all the rooms and apartments I have occupied in various cities and countries, I duly developed an almost infallible ear for his arrival—the central event of my day, around which all else revolves.

In the small Massachusetts town where I languished for four long years in training to be a bachelor of nebulous arts, the metal mailbox lid generally clinked at ten o'clock, give or take fifteen minutes, and it would have been futile to register for a nine o'clock class since nothing but that clink—like the chuck wagon come-'n-get-it clang of the Wild West—could possibly rustle me awake.

When the mailman came early, say at eight o'clock, as he did in the old walled bishopric in the Black Forest in Germany (where I went to study fairy tales), my day began with the squeak of his rubber-soled shoes on the freshly polished parquet floor in the lobby of my rooming house,

and the suction effect of his first opening then shutting
the downstairs door, which carried molecule by molecule
the three flights up the winding funnel of air to my room
at the head of the stairs, made my door rattle softly and
my windowpanes tinkle.

In Vienna, where I spent an unhappy year as a would-
be novelist in search of a plot, the vestibule floor of my
dingy fin-de-siècle flophouse was imperial marble, and the
mailman's forbidding steps echoed at half past ten on
weekdays and a quarter to eleven every Saturday, rudely
intruding on my dreams.

And here in lower Manhattan, in the three-story walk-
up on the fourth floor of which (converted attic) I have
loitered legally for more than a decade, the mailman arrives
sometimes at half past noon, sometimes at one, sometimes
never at all, his arrival announced by the barking chorus
of the mad woman's dogs downstairs. My sleeping habits
have changed accordingly, and I now rise sometimes at half
past twelve, sometimes at one, sometimes never at all.

Lying in bed, in a trance of anticipation on those days
when the mailman is late, it would be difficult to measure
the level of longing that consumes me. It is not that I feel
particularly lonely. There are people I see and with whom
I talk from time to time on the telephone. I enjoy the
conversations and encounters. But there is something altogether different about the kind of communion that awaits
you flat and folded, stamped and sealed in an envelope.

Who will, or will anyone write to me today? I wonder.

Awake, eyelids as yet unopened (the eyes are envel-
opes unto themselves), I mull over all the people I know
or have known, those loved, those liked and those unfit for
words. Sweet is the possibility of news from a friend or the
thoughtful wellwishes of an old acquaintance fallen out of

touch, and every aspiring writer hopes that the day's mail may bring a letter from a publisher. Sweeter still is the anticipation of a love letter: the imagined pressure of a hand pushing a pen across the page, tracing waves of passion, and the gaps when language falters . . . telling by not telling. With a writer's peculiar craving for separation from the object of his desire, I savor the distance and taste the glue of that triangle licked shut.

But the sweetest suspense of all—and here I must confess to the betrayal inherent in a lifelong cultivation of dreams—attends the possible receipt of a letter from an unknown, perhaps even anonymous sender. My longing for such a letter taps the very wellspring of my being and is the strongest passion of which I am capable. For this letter that may never come (and whose arrival I dread as much as I desire) I have been waiting all my life and will continue to wait and listen for intently at the approach of the mailman, a mere civil servant to some, the winged angel of my private apocalypse.

Poor
Jimmy Somebody

As the first flakes of snow started to fall, Eleanor remembered other snowfalls in other places. The snow always made her sad because there was something final about it and because it made everything look like a beautiful cemetary. She stared out the window.—"I feel like the Statue of Liberty," she said, thinking aloud.

"What, hun?" Steve muttered.

"Like the Statue of Liberty," she repeated, annoyed at herself for having put such an odd feeling into words, but wanting nonetheless to complete the picture:—"the kind they put in paperweights where when you shake them the snow starts falling."

"Salami's on sale," Steve reported, folding the newspaper he was studying.

"When I was a little girl," Eleanor continued, talking more to herself than to Steve, "I felt so sorry for her. There she is, I thought, Liberty locked forever inside that stupid paperweight with the same snow always falling, and she can't ever get out—"

"What do you say we turn on the tv, sweetheart," Steve suggested, "I bet there's a good old movie on."

"It must be awful to feel closed in like that!" Eleanor mused.

"I could go for a Gary Cooper," Steve persisted, "or a—what's his name?—you know, the other guy, the guy I always get mixed up with Gary Cooper?"

"Steve—?!"

"What is it, darling?"

"You don't think I'm like her, do you!?"

"Like who?"

"Like Liberty inside a paperweight."

"What kind of crazy idea is that!"

"I found two new gray hairs today, Steve—there's hardly any black left."

"I told you to dye it!"

"But I don't want to dye it, Steve. If my hair is gray, I want to see it the way it is."

"That's silly, honey—this is America, nothing's the way it is—you know you'll always be my little sweet sixteen!"

"But I'm not sixteen anymore, Steve!"

"It's not how old you are, sweetheart, it's how old you *feel!*"

"I'm thirty-nine, Steve, a thirty-nine-year-old Statue of Liberty inside a paperweight."

"Nonsense!" Steve puckered his lips, stretching out his arms to her—"You're my snukkums Elly-pooh and I'm your cuddly-wuddly . . ."

"Don't talk like that, Steve!" Eleanor cut him short, "I can't stand it when you talk like that!"

"Well aren't we Miss Serious today!" Steve smiled uncomfortably. "Honestly, Elly, I don't know what's gotten into you all of a sudden. I mean, it's Sunday afternoon, for Christ sake,—save the gloomies for Monday morning!''

"You're right, Steve,'' Eleanor conceded, regretting having started in on this track to begin with. Silence is golden, she said to herself, and then for no reason in particular she swung around and opened the closet door.

"What are you doing, honey?'' Steve asked.

"I'm going for a walk,'' she announced, though the idea had only just occurred to her as she reached for her cap and coat.

"It's snowing out!'' Steve protested.

"I know,'' she said, slipping into one coat sleeve and then the other.

"Be sensible,'' he insisted, "this is no time to go for a walk!''

Eleanor pulled the red woollen cap down over her ears. "I'll be back . . . *soon*,'' she said, addressing his bewildered reflection in the mirror on the inside of the closet door.

"I bet there's a good old movie on,'' Steve tried to coax her, "they usually show good movies Sunday afternoon, that's when *most* people want to stay home!''

Eleanor shut the closet and walked toward the door.

"Okaaaaay!'' Steve sighed, rising reluctantly from his armchair, "I'll get my coat.''

"No!'' she declared.

"What on earth has gotten into you, Elly! This isn't like you at all. Is it that time of the month?''

Eleanor bit her lips, trying hard to hold back a scream: "Please, Stephen,'' she said.

"Stephen!?—Who's Stephen?—This is your husband Steve, remember me?''

"It's the snow,'' she tried to explain, "it makes me terribly sad.''

"That's crazy, the snow is beautiful,'' he said, "it ought

to make you feel young and alive! Me, I'd like to go out right now and build a snowman—what do you say, Elly?"

"It's like a cemetary when it snows . . ."

"What kind of thing to say is that!? You'd think you were a hundred years old or something!"

"I feel a hundred years old, I feel as old as the earth and all the people buried under all the snowfalls,—" Eleanor paused, she might have said more, might have tried somehow to put it into words, but then she turned to look at him, and their eyes met like the beams of two cars approaching and passing in the night.

"Okay," he said—there was nothing else to say—and sank back wearily into the armchair.

Eleanor flung open the front door and sucked in a deep breath of air. She stuck out her tongue to taste the snow, but it didn't taste like anything. She turned around again to look at her husband. He had already switched on the tv and his eyes were glued to the screen. There was a movie on, one she'd seen before, one with that other guy, not Gary Cooper,—Billy, Bobby, Jimmy somebody. Snow was falling in the movie too and the story came back to her in a flash, about a sincere, honest, upstanding young man who lived in a small town and always wanted to get out, only he never does, and the movie was supposed to make you feel in the end that it was the best thing for him that he never got out, but she knew it was a lie, felt it inside like a suffocating sadness.—"Poor Jimmy Somebody," she whispered, and then suddenly remembering his name: "Poor Jimmy Stewart!"

"What's that, dear?" Steve asked, but his voice sounded muffled, faraway, like it came from the glass-enclosed world of the tv snowstorm.

"Poor Jimmy Stewart," she muttered, "poor Steve, poor

Liberty . . ." And the words melted into tears, a quiet whimper at first, that broke little by little into uncontrollable spasms of sobbing. Something was cracking, some invisible wall was giving way, on the other side of which she could already feel the cool fresh air of an open place, a place she'd never been to but which she could remember like you remember Eden.

"Honey," he said, "It's a Wonderful Life is on, with Jimmy Stewart—you remember."

She slammed the door behind her and ran out into the snow.

II. MICROTALES

1. URBAN FAUNA

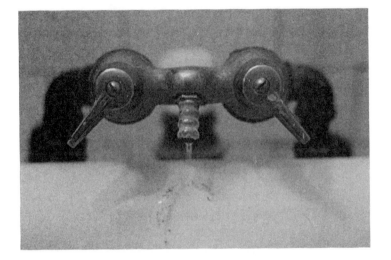

Pigeons

There is something comic, chaplinesque in a pigeon's walk. Head bobbing, ridiculously pecking as though at an invisible seed or crumb, it waddles forward, ever onwards, ever hopeful. With its three-pronged feet (plus one absurd vestigial hind toe) it resembles a court jester, a resemblance enhanced by the violet and blue iridescence of its feather cloak. To lonely old women it embodies the hungry incarnation of their lost or never found love, and will stick around as long as the bread holds out. When finally it takes flight, awkward and heavy, this asphalt-colored bird is like a piece of the pavement which by some fluke of gravity broke loose and is foolishly falling upwards by mistake.

Sea Gulls

Sea gulls belong to the clouds. Fallen splinters of eternity, they hang overhead with the equanimity and mild disdain of angels in a medieval altarpiece, and unlike pigeons, refuse any contact with man. Being a white body with wings, the sea gull naturally taps a sentimental streak—poets beware! Its terrestrial counterpart is not the soul, but a white paper bag blowing aimlessly along the curb.

Beware of Cat

Dogs and cats employ their tails quite differently in ways that punctuate their diverse spirits. Both are flexible extensions of the spine: South Pole to the North Pole of animal intellect, but this is where the likeness ends. The canine tail wags and points insistently, the feline insinuates with a sultry curl. For the cat is a question and the dog is a statement. The cat conjures up Egyptian mysteries, the dog echoes the brash bark of Rome. Cave Canem! Beware of Dog! Yet never do they warn of the incalculable claws of the cat. Hercules slipped past Cerberus unscathed, while the Sphinx was Oedipus' ruin. All this is signalled in the twist of their tails.

Subway Mice

Subway mice—true urbanites—wear coats of khaki rather than gray, ever ready for war. Attacks come unpredictably every five, ten, fifteen minutes: a roar in the tunnel from which the desperate guerillas take cover where they can: savvy old veterans in the gaps between pillars, leaping clear of the current; and the foolhardy new recruits in crevices between the tracks and ties, where the casualties are more severe. Some refuse to run. Perhaps their hunger is too great, or their strength has failed them, or a stubborn resolve not to be mistaken for suicide suddenly takes hold. It may be a tin can bleeding sweetly, or a bread rind, or the irresistible allure of a brown paper bag. Playing hide and seek with fate, their tiny tails flap—oblivious to the rumble and the ominous pair of yellow eyes grinning in the distance.

Squirrels

Beloved for the falling-leaf-like way it moves, the squirrel may beg a nut, but disdains any further interaction with man. The rat revolts us because it comes too close, invading our habitats, intruding even in our dreams. Not so the squirrel. More of a dwarf-deer than a rodent (its home being not the sewer but the lawn), it is a permanent visitor in the city, a reluctant resident. If in one respect, namely its tendency to hoard, it resembles us, the squirrel is quick to dispel any other possible parallels. With a sudden vertical pivot, as if to prove that the law of gravity does not pertain to it, the squirrel leaps clear of human limitations. Scampering up a tree and bounding effortlessly from branch to branch, it sometimes seems to be laughing at us.

Still Life

The brush attracts attention to itself by dipping its
bristles in red paint. You drew me that way before, the
subject, a hand, protests. But the brush, oblivious to such
premature criticism, paints a big red circle, almost a circle
but not quite. What's that supposed to be? the subject
wants to know, jealous as always of not being the center
of attention. The brush drips its bristles in white paint this
time and splatters the hand. The anxious fingers, relieved
for the time being, shut up and watch. Now the brush dips
its bristles in green paint. Green, says the whitewashed
hand, so this is going to be a still life. When the brush
paints the subject's fingernails green, the subject is mo-
mentarily stunned. That was unexpected, very interesting.
Meanwhile, the red not-quite-but-almost circle is growing
restless and starts whistling at the brush. You'll never attract its attention that way, the subject says. Just be yourself, it says, the brush likes things that are themselves. The
would-be circle is still again. This was a ploy on the sub-

ject's part to detract attention from anything but itself. The brush can't stand such vanity. It dips its bristles in black and spins madly in a kind of St. Vitus Dance, splattering black all about, ignoring both the hand and the disconsolate unfinished circle. What kind of dumb prima donna thing to do is that, the subject complains. The circle is sulking. Still the brush won't stop spinning. The black droplets that it scatters grow ever finer and become a mist, and before you know it, it has dipped itself into and is dripping red again. A slow fat red this time. The subject is scandalized and also fiercely jealous. You don't know what you're doing. The brush sends a fat glob of red flying. It lands somewhere out of sight. Delighted, the brush does it again, this time with green again. The hand, still dripping white, is frightened out of its wits and crawls for safety inside the circle, almost inside but not quite. This in fact is what the brush, by subtle conniving, has been waiting for. The painting is complete, almost.

Balloon Envy

So puffed up, so superior—the bearing of a new balloon borders on arrogance. And were it not for the enticing way it beckons you to tug on its ribbon tail and the lusty bounce with which it responds, you would be sorely tempted to abandon it to the blue yonder or in a fit of rage, to reply with the prick of a scissor tip. Instead, you indulge its whims, toy with it, caress it, press it, squeeze it, tap it, slap it around the room, give it all the attention it craves. Like a caged bird, the balloon defies confinement and can never really be possessed. Fickle thing, it would just as soon bounce and dangle its tail for another. And who can resist its firm shape and the seductive lure of such lightness? Hold and let go, hold and let go . . . The game is repeated till either or both of the partners grow tired, release, and rise or fall respectively into their separate repose. Adulation is sweet, but age comes quickly to a balloon. The form you found so irresistible last night lies shrivelled and feeble on the floor the next morning in a tangle of ribbon, stretch marks radiating around its once alluring nipple. A shadow of its former self, it flies now only when you kick it.

Little Alien from the Planet Uterus

These spots and swirls resembling lunar scapes (transmitted, not from Outer, but from Inner Space) reveal the molten core of the Planet Uterus, its sole inhabitant soon to erupt, kicking up a cosmic storm, refusing to hold still for identification. The technician takes a fuzzy likeness all the same. What will it want? What will earth look like on landing, its population towering perilously overhead? Read this years hence, little alien from the Planet Uterus, and remember—your mother, her bulging belly being prodded by a hightech cattle prong; your father, benumbed bull peering fearfully over the technician's shoulder, asking: What is it?; and you, a reluctant neuter squiggle on a screen, a black hole, a big bang in the making—Is there pleasure and pain where you are?

Apocryphal Sightings

Like the dry shed skins found lying on the forest bed or footprints fossilized by time—consider the solitary sheath and chain wrapped round a mangled relic found clinging to a lamppost on a barren streetcorner. These are the bones of the urban desert. Jackals have been here, buzzards have pecked out the eyes and other identifying features. It is impossible to say for certain what it was, yet as with the huddled human husks of Pompei and Herculaneum, there is evidence here of a stubborn holding on up until the very last, a refusal to yield despite the pressure of an overpowering force.

Singing Doors

Its preliminary protest upon being roused resembles a yawn. But push or pull it open to its widest angle of aperture and the sound swells into a full-fledged lament (the pitch and volume of which depend on just how unhinged it is at the moment, and whether you are serious about departure or simply putting out the rubbish). A door with which you have lived a long time can sense your intentions by the swing of your step and the relative pressure of your grip on its knob. Is the underlying emotion genuine, or is the door merely being theatrical, playing its part, asserting its independence from the wall? This we may never know. But the fact remains that, staged or real, there is no wail in nature at once so heart-rending and so stirring as the high-C soprano of a door slammed shut. In that un-oiled instance of anguish, the door gives all before rejoining the dull domestic harmony of the wall, and you could swear you heard it cry out your name with the ardor of a forsaken lover and the undying devotion of the mother whom every man must abandon.

2. BIOCHIPS

"Nude"

ı.
ı, an.
dscape.
ıil paintı.
smaller
.ills, and
urch's ł
ı elsewł
. life-siz
ıtub to
:oncer
attan
apocaly
.bove and
ers on the .
ı the subway
ıistic pranks
ıle while the su
ll are treated
high-keyed wa:
tify as the sec
Expressionisı
e that, it is b
ities of his (
ı in cityscaı
paintings
y the w
– woulı
'. Wh
rol,
ha

Cornell Listening to a Box of Rice Krispies

Cornell, listening to a box of Rice Krispies, overheard what no man was meant to hear. Snap, Crackle and Pop had had it. They were through being commercial mouthpieces. They were through grinning innocently, good-naturedly for the boys and girls. It was their stifled libidos acting up, and Cornell, marooned in the wilds of Queens, sympathized. The sounds he heard upon shaking the box were obscene, desperate, and he shook on. What are you up to, Joseph, asked his mother from the kitchen. Listening to Rice Krispies, he said. Funny sons I have, thought his mother, I wonder why. The more he shook the box, the more agitated the sounds became. Are you dying, whispered Cornell. But the desperate sounds did not abate. And Cornell kept shaking the box. Then his brother came in with a kitchen knife and stuck it in the box. There, said his brother, they'll be quiet now. Thank you, said Cornell, I didn't have the guts to do it myself. You're welcome, said his brother, who never said another word.

Thank You, Marcel Duchamp

The skin in the televised interview with Duchamp is lined like the palm of a hand. Discovery: he is a hand. He twitches his eyebrows and sucks his cigar. Eventually the interview is over and he dies. Thank you, Marcel Duchamp. Well, I'm delighted, his deceased image sighs.

Are There Any Catfish in the Thames?

Dear Reginald, wrote Twain to his boyhood friend Reginald Tweedham, whom he had not seen in decades. I lie in bed and can neither rise nor recline. The wife has taken the little Clemens for an outing and left the old scribbler back home to brood. I am supposed to compose another book, preferably for boys, but I am mightily weary of all that innocence. We've been through it, Tweedham, you and I, caught catfish together and plucked out their whiskers, muddled through from the impatience of boyhood to the weariness of age. I have no stories left to tell. None but the tale of an old dreamer propped up in bed remembering better days, no, not better days, Tweedham, bygone days with the misery bleached out. No notion of where life has taken you, but I'll post this note to your kin in London and hope it reaches you. Are there any catfish in the Thames? Your friend, Samuel.

Ibsen's Hat

Henrik Ibsen never went anywhere without his hat. Refusing to entrust it to a hatcheck's charge, he preferred to place it beside him, always requisitioning an empty seat at whatever cost. Its positioning was crucial and the dramatist took great pains to tilt it just right. The significance of the hat, a mystery heretofore, was only recently revealed when a packet of the playwright's letters were sold at Sotheby's. "I spotted you this afternoon in the crook of my hat," he addressed a correspondent by the initial N (thought by some to have inspired Nora). Apparently flattered by the famous man's attention, N must have challenged him to explain. For another note dated the following day reads: "Man must protect himself from beauty's Medusa gaze. Do tell me where you plan to sit at tomorrow's performance. I prefer pearl earrings." And yet another note concludes: "The cad, the fool, the critic T rushing to congratulate me for yesterday's premiere of P.G. (probably *Peer Gynt*) knocked over my doffer and smashed my second set of

eyes. Will have to love you blindly 'til I find a replacement."
Ibsen, it seems, wore a pocket mirror tucked into the sweat-
band of his hat—which explains an obscure line crossed
out in the original manuscript of A *Doll's House*: "Only en-
closed by glass does beauty arouse manageable emotions."

Goethe

I was a stone bust of the great poet Goethe riding among bleeding sides of beef in a butcher's freezer truck.

The Notebooks of
Fantom Chekhov

On the shelf, a book that wrenches my eye out of its socket: *The Notebooks of Fantom Chekhov*. No, I know what you're thinking, that the eye plays tricks and sees ridiculous things. I look again. No mistake about it. It isn't Anton, the illustrious playwright and short story master, but another man who merely shares his name. Nothing about him, it says in the foreword, is known other than the fact that he kept these notebooks throughout an apparently lonely and uneventful life. He never went to Siberia, never got into trouble with the censors, never troubled the conscience of his time. But Fantom did not despair. The wife he never married made no demands. The children he never bore never badgered him for money. Through it all, Fantom maintained his belief in—well, belief is a big word—he stuck by his pencil. A pencil is a quiet man's best friend, he wrote in the notable first page of his notebook, date and place unknown. The rest of the page is empty. Indecision? Sterility? Perhaps. Fantom makes repeated reference to what he calls *holding tactics*. Such tactics are helpful, he writes, when confronting sunsets. Let other men say: Look, how lovely! I say: Bosh! Sunrises are easier to deal with, largely because we sleep through them. Other memorable passages deride *the forced grin we bear in the face of beauty and originality*. I am ordinary, writes Chekhov, and I like it that way. The special man admires himself in the mirror of his words and actions. He needs to be petted and have his high self-regard upheld by others. The ordinary man needs nothing. His skin fits. There is one brief biographical note on page 56 of the second notebook, though the allusion may be imagined: *My mother wanted to call me Fiodor, but my father said No! Call him Fantom, it will serve him well in the hollow life that lies ahead*. This appears to raise the possibility that Fantom's father might have been a Russian Nihilist, but he might also simply have been a depressed practical joker. The notebooks end on a sardonic note: *I have broken my pencil point and cannot continue . . .* The manuscript was discovered, so we read in the foreword, in a garbage bin in the basement of the library of the Hermitage on the eve of the Revolution. Fantom, the editor conjectures, was either a librarian or a janitor with a wry sense of humor. Or else he was somebody else.

The Flesh of
Non-Existent Women

The poet Peter Altenberg gripped the frames of his spectacles, wavering between the urge to crush them and to slip them into his inside pocket. Portable windows, he called them and laughingly imagined replacing the lenses with stained shards stolen from the Sainte Chapelle. It would lend me, he would tell his friends, a more colorful imagination. He took out a pen to jot down the thought, but the weight of the gold-tipped fountain pen (a gift from a female admirer) was suddenly more than he could bear, and besides, he had no paper. Waiter, he called, bring me another schnapps. It was his fifth of the afternoon. Another could not hurt and perhaps it would loosen the tightness he felt in his brain. In a dream the night before, he had witnessed the digging of the Erie Canal, watched nubile young girls obliged to ride naked and bareback on Indian elephants drawing barges behind. He awakened to the frightening spectacle of their revolt, girls and elephants charging at him out of his sweat-soaked pillow. Waiter, he called, bring me a sheet of paper. I want to note down how curious it is to feel the flesh of non-existent women. The waiter shook his head and smiled, accustomed to the habits of the poet.

Laederach with Coca Cola and Swallow in New York

Picture this. Laederach on a midtown streetcorner. The towering Swiss author sipping Coca Cola through a straw and complaining that the stuff is too sweet. Photographer stationed below with head tilted back considering the dizzying height of his subject. Laederach is obliged to stand still as a statue, no easy task for a man of such magnitude. You can talk, the photographer allows, taking light readings, establishing the optimal angle, but don't budge. A brooding giraffe in the asphalt jungle, the Swiss author slowly slurps his drink, surveying the minuscule population of the American metropolis, all the while chewing over sundry thoughts. The photographer first tries to shoot the subject up the right pants leg, but the knee obstructs the face. The left leg, on the other hand, offers a somewhat more auspicious vista. Now all they have to do is wait for a particularly dense cloud blocking the sun to pass. But in the meantime, a tour bus has pulled up along the curb; the man with the microphone apparently mistook the tall fellow having his picture taken for a famous sports celebrity. A brash behemoth in plaid pants and a platinum perm emerges from the bus holding forth the program of the long-running musical A *Chorus Line* and an Empire State Building-shaped ballpoint, soliciting an autograph for her Timmy back in Fort Wayne. Timmy has cancer, she says, and would be thrilled to death with the autograph of a New York Giant. Sorry, lady, Laederach says, I'm no athlete, just an author, but I'd be happy to sign all the same for Timmy's sake. The behemoth angrily rips pen and program out of the author's hands. Some people! she fumes and marches back to the bus. Meanwhile, the cloud has lifted and the light is perfect, couldn't be better. Ready, says the photographer, adjusting his settings. Just then a swallow lands on the shoulder of the Swiss. A pigeon would be more appropriate, Laederach, who has still not reached the bottom of his jumbo coke, remarks. As a boy, he says, I was always afraid of birds. An aunt of mine once threatened: If you don't behave, my canary will pluck out your eyes. At the time I had been reading Sophocles's Oedipus cycle. The prospect of being blinded simultaneously terrified and thrilled me. By the way, Laederach adds, Marianne can't stand the sound of birds chirping, the twitter disturbs her musical balance, keeps her from concentrating on the keys. No artist takes competition kindly. Beneath him, Laederach feels the rumble of commuters. The (canned) bells of St. Patrick's or some other church chime five o'clock. Another dark cloud overhead. Doesn't look like we're going to get to it today, I'm afraid, the photographer shrugs, maybe tomorrow.

Attila the Tailor

It's true, there is a man who rides his needle as ruth-lessly, as skillfully, as artfully as Attila the Hun rode his horse. To him, a linen suit is the barren and beautiful tundra across which he flies, barely touching the material lest his fingers leave a mark. He is brutal with the pleats and cuffs—the fabric must obey or else be cut off—and yet he knows and respects the treachery of linen, the susceptibility of silk. Beware, he will whisper to a customer whose belly bulges the waistband. With linen I can give you no more. For Attila is an aging warrior, his grand campaigns cross worsted wool and herring bone behind him now. He has weathered the onslaught of synthetics and learned to live with it. Soon, says Attila, I will put away my needle for good and let the younger men lay down their chalk track. But they will remember me, he says, for the speed of my needle, the daring of my eye, and the precision of my scissors.

Another Jewish Magician

Hanging upside-down, Houdini thought of many things. How the crowd of onlookers hung like flies in the flypaper of their fear. How the skyscrapers dangled like stalagmites and everything looked like its reflection. He thought a moment of Christ on the cross, another Jewish magician famed for his ability to get out of tight fixes. He knew that the crowd loved him only so long as he did not falter and yet they half-hoped he would. The one thing he failed to consider until it was too late was the gold watch he'd neglected to remove from his vest pocket when the workmen hoisted him head over heels, the timepiece that now slowly wormed its way out, dangled an instant and dropped into the mud below. From now on, Houdini decided, I'll wear a watch chain.

The Birdman

Mr. Lang lives alone. Not really alone, just without any human involvements. He loves birds and calls them his children. His home is full of flying children. Day and night you can hear a happy twitter.

And the children love their Uncle Lang. He lays breadcrumbs and grass seed for them on his waxed bald head; and they fly down, land, and try to eat while standing still, whereupon their little claws slide as on a dance floor, and draw thin red lines—blood hairs, Mr. Lang likes to call them.

And evenings when it's time to go to sleep, Mr. Lang puts two little birds into a little cage. He takes the cage with him into the kitchen. The birds chirp merrily until all of a sudden they give off a panicked shriek. "Silence, children!" screams Mr. Lang.

Quickly he opens the cage gate, sticks his hand in, grabs one after the other, and flings them into the modern gas range with the wide view glass door. He presses a button and the oven light goes on. The birds fly wildly about.

"Have no fear, children!" he whispers and taps softly with his fingers on the glass. With the other hand he turns on the gas. He sets himself a stool in front of the oven. With swelling excitement he watches.

Seated so he finally falls asleep and dreams of woods and meadows, of Birkenau, where he worked as a young technician. Children fly up to heaven in his dream. They smile and wave to him.

The Two Collectors

Two men lived in the same city. Their paths in life would never have crossed had it not been for the incident that I am about to narrate. The one was a dealer in rare prints and drawings of the old masters. He was rich and respected by his fellow dealers. The other, recently released from a state mental institution, wheeled a shopping cart full of paper and cellophane wrappings up and down the street. He cared for nothing but wrappings.

One day the art dealer was arrested for fraud. It seems that his Rembrandts were in fact Riley originals and that his Goya prints were done by the same Mr. Riley. For the first time in his life, the elegant dealer found himself behind bars, sharing his cell with none other than the wrappings collector who had been picked up that same day for vagrancy.

Now in this world there are certain types of people: the scribblers who record life in books or on bathroom walls; the actors, who crave an audience whether from stage

189

or street corner; the critics, who cannot help but criticize;—
and then there are the collectors, who out of a primal need,
search out certain select commodities for the sole purpose
of possessing them.

At first the art dealer was horrified by his vagrant cell-
mate. But when he observed the love and care with which
the other man sorted and folded cigarette pack celophanes
and the wrappings of toilet paper rolls, he began to feel a
sense of kinship. The art dealer was truly sad when the
vagrant's sentence was up. They had never talked with each
other. The night before he was to be released, the vagrant,
without a word, handed the dealer his shoebox full of the
wrappings he'd collected while in prison. And as there were
no rare prints and drawings to buy and sell, the art dealer
took up the collection.

After his designated sentence had come to an end,
the dealer traveled all over the world in search of wrappings
both plain and exotic: tissue paper, skins and embroidered
silk. He opened a gallery and soon grew rich again. Then
came the Depression. Wealthy buyers of exotica vanished
from one day to the next. The gallery was foreclosed and
the dealer turned out of his penthouse apartment.

Now I don't know if it's the same two men, but I have
seen two vagrants together wheeling shopping carts full of
paper and cellophane down the street. How they found
each other again (if it is indeed them) is a mystery. But
collectors are a mysterious sort, and I am a scribbler and
cannot help but record what I see.

Mirage

If a picture is worth a thousand words (to risk a time-worn truism), then a word is worth one one-thousandth of a picture: find the missing nine hundred and ninety-nine pieces, set each in its proper place, and the picture is complete.

Such were the thoughts that sparked the already feverish brain of the late Graham T. Nesbit, as he crouched unwisely in the full noon glare of the North African sun, shooing away flies with one hand, and delicately fingering with the other a tiny chip of human bone, engraved with a single unfamiliar symbol.

Professor Nesbit was elated as only an archeologist can be, who, after digging digging for a decade at the same site, and turning up nothing but pieces of pots and more pots, finally stumbles on a significant find. This sandy hill had become his life. He liked to think he knew it better than any man can know his garden or his wife. Every day for the last ten years, at dawn and then again at sunset, he circled that hill, caressed it with his eyes the way a man caresses the body of his beloved, and watched its thin dry yellow grass waving like hair in the wind.

That night when the old professor crawled into his tent, he was indeed elated.

What did it mean, that symbol scratched into human bone? Could this be a language, a clue to an entire civilization as yet unknown to scholars?

He was not a man given to sudden bursts of revelation. Archeologists are generally sober, patient visionaries. Though stone dry on the surface, their passion creeps like a snake over sand and time.

As a boy, Graham Nesbit loved puzzles. On one occasion he had sat for more than a year over the most complex, five thousand piece puzzle of the Parthenon until it was all there. And as a grown man the same patience served him well to reassemble pots and languages. But on this occasion the North African sun hammering down all day left its mark. Professor Nesbit, who normally took such care to seek shelter at regular intervals and especially at noon, had abandoned all sensible precautions, lost in silent revery on a chip of bone. Now he suffered the consequences.

Fever fed the old professor's secret phantasy.

A city sprouted from the hill. High clay walls glistening white. Sun baked streets. Shadowy commerce. Dark draped women, veils flapping in the wind. Children, laughter and the persistent cry of spice vendors.

The words were indecipherable but the meaning was clear. Here was the supreme puzzle, all put together, no missing pieces, complete and yet as much a puzzle as it would ever be. The old archeologist wept for he knew that he would never enter that city, and that in searching for it all these years in his sober, scholarly way, he had been blind to the gates of another place, gates that were now slowly swinging shut.

The Princess Angeline

It is fashionable nowadays to deny one's true age, to bleach away the gray and stretch the wrinkles. Not so the Princess Angeline. When last interviewed she proudly asserted a century of residence on this earth. Were they happy times? Bah, says the Princess, I had my moments. And what is her most vivid memory? She pauses to shoo away a persistent fly. Well, she said, I really can't remember. Has she seen the Hand of Progress boldly forge ahead? Would the man with the pencil please repeat the question! The Princess admits that her two favorite inventions are the rocking chair and the window seat of a speeding iron horse. I like motion, she smiles.

The Cigarette Swallower

There was once a cigarette swallower who performed his extraordinary act on the Rue de la Harpe. Everyone watched in amazement as this skeleton of a man devoured Gauloises and even the stronger Moroccan imports as though they were the finest delicacies.

He stuck out his long lizard tongue and lay the thin white cylinders flat against it, so that a glowing tobacco eye peered at the onlookers up until the last second. Then he winked slyly and with acrobatic ease, tumbled the cigarette once over backwards, blew a perfect smoke ring, and like a predator, greedily swallowed his still living prey.

And when the blasé drunken crowd threatened to grow weary of such wonders, lured by the seductive flute of the snake charmer on the next corner, then the cigarette swallower held up a sparkling razor blade. Open-mouthed, the crowd lingered for one last long second, hoping for—well maybe, just a drop of blood.

He grinned, gave proof on his bony arm that indeed

195

the blade could cut; and then, with cold desire, ran his tongue along both edges, let it embrace the blade like any eager Casanova, and swiftly drew the tender morsel into his mouth. A forefinger crossed tightly clasped lips to demand silence. Without a sound, his protruding adam's apple rose and fell. Everyone felt the blade as though sliding down their own throat; no one doubted the authenticity of this miracle.

You froze in the short flash of a shiver, like when you accidentally catch a glimpse of a private scene on a dark street corner or in a lighted window, stop and stare, oblivious to propriety, until sirens or other street sounds shake you out of your trance. Ashamed then you rush off to catch other attractions of the night.

Expensive Dentistry
and Muscle Control

G. J. Joseph, the popular crooner, whose soft melli-
fluous voice soothes raw nerves in elevators and offices
and drowns out the piercing shriek of the dentist's drill,
lives surrounded by fish. He owns a glass-bottom boat
which he keeps docked in Naples (Florida), and has
boarded only once (afraid as he is of the ocean), and
a lavish triplex on Manhattan's East Side, the walls of
which are lined with an intricate system of connecting
fish tanks inhabited by an assortment of the exotic and
the ordinary: an electric eel named Neon that glows at
night and saves electricity, blow fish (his favorite named
Satchmo, whose bloated belly reminds the singer of the
cheeks of the famous trumpeteer), minnows, swordfish,
stingrays, and countless other fish, including a shark
which he keeps confined in the walls around his oval-
shaped bed and which he personally likes to feed when

he is not on tour. G. J. sings of love in a way that touches the heartstrings of Middle America. His smile on album covers and at live performances is appealing but unthreatening, itself the product of expensive dentistry and muscle control.

The Presidents of Argentina

I was born in a coffin, the new President of Argentina joked with a chuckle to his recently deposed adversary, twirling the pointed ends of his black mustache. Believe me, I know what it's like to die! he grinned. Then he lowered his arm, but instead of firing on the prisoner, the guards pivoted and fired on him. Newspapers formerly of the governing party, then of the opposition, now once again voicing the official view, reported that the President had been reinstated, and the traitor executed. His body hacked into three pieces so that it would fit neatly into a tiny two-foot coffin, to save wood and space.

I Will Be
Your Umbrella, Darling,
I Will Be
Your Chandelier!

This I can tell you, Machnof, the beautiful midget Chiquita whispered into the ear of the giant, Altitude is relative. A table top gives me vertigo. Last night I dreamt I was your hat and you doffed me to the King of Spain, who wept because I was so beautiful, and because he could not have me. I too suffer, the giant replied. My mother and father, perfectly normal Russian peasants, abandoned me because I was too big, and the effort to feed me even as an infant was more than they could bear. I became a household mascot for the master's children. Once Count Tolstoy came to visit; it was before he had made a name for himself with his big books. Life wearies me, Machnof, he said. You need to participate more, I told him, not hide from it in a mouthful of pretty phrases. Listen to me, Machnof, said Chiquita. Tonight let me sleep in your shoe so that I may sense what it is like to tread like a mountain. Machnof sighed. These many years you have known me, performed at my side, displayed your bare heart to those who think themselves normal, and still you never suspected . . . He broke into tears. Chiquita comforted him. I will be your umbrella, darling, I will be your chandelier!

3. REFRACTIONS

How to Kill Time

It is not enough to merely strangle time. There's too much of it for that, and the very element you thought to release from its misery will tackle you in turn and do you in. Try if you like to crush a second, noisome mosquito,—a swarm of others will sting you in its wake and make you wish you were no longer that swollen aching mass of me.

I have tried to drown it, asphyxiate it, disembowel and decapitate (all the medieval techniques), and even to deny its existence—nothing doing!

The only effective method I have found for temporarily immobilizing (if not obliterating) time is to take pleasure in its passing.

* * *

Adore it, lie with it, give it the face of your lover.

Make a pet of it, if that pleases you, and walk it on a leash.
    Play shafts of time like pick-up sticks.
    Engage in discourse, chess, sodomy—anything to keep
it occupied.

An idle hour is a viscious hour.

The Swiss and Japanese have refined the art of taming it
in tiny mechanical circuses.
    Wait a minute, you cry, craving a respite, and already
the thing you thought to keep at bay has turned on you
and dug its fangs into your flesh.
    The venom works quickly, paralyzing its victim.

Helpless, you lie there, as the terrible tide of eternity rises
around you . . .

The Dangling Avalanche

He was a schoolteacher and liked to make up story titles in his spare time. The stories might follow, but it made no difference if they didn't. A good title says it all. He would match up favorite words and note down new combinations. Today it was "avalanche" (reminiscent of the TV westerns of his black-and-white childhood) and "dangling" (as in "dangling participle," the grammarian's bugbear). Together the two made a splendid couple, he thought, one of his finest creations to date: "The Dangling Avalanche," the story of a catastrophe that hadn't yet happened, though it might at any moment.

What a title I have for you today! he said on the phone to his friend, a short story writer who had been suffering from a prolonged bout of writer's block. Tell me! said the friend, chewed pencil stub in hand. The Dan-gling Av-a-lanche, the schoolteacher proudly declaimed, savoring each syllable. Not bad, his friend replied, and following the

207

requisite courtesies, hung up and turned to his typewriter and wrote:

A man and a woman went riding through a canyon.

The writer paused, read the sentence aloud to himself, liked it and continued:

The man spurred on his mule, eager to traverse the canyon quickly.

The boulders perched precariously overhead made him nervous.

The woman looked up. Mira, Juan! she said, How lovely, that ribbon of blue!

Yes, the man grunted, his eyes on the path.

Wait! urged the woman, we have all day—no sense rushing back. At this point the writer was interrupted by a knock at the door. It was his neighbor, a popular novelist who came ostensibly to borrow sugar, but in actual point of fact had a book contract to fulfill and not the faintest idea of where to begin.—I need your help, the novelist confessed and proceeded to explain his dilemma, offering handsome payment in exchange for a plot.

Sit down! said the short story writer, too destitute to turn down such a tempting offer, and poured his neighbor a cup of strong coffee. Now listen, he said, and he read him the minuscule fragment.

And—? asked the novelist—What next? Did they stop to make love? Did the rocks fall and crush them? Or did the journey continue uneventfully?

Nothing of the sort! the short story writer smiled. She wanted to stop and look up at the sky. He wanted to ride on. And the rocks wanted to fall. Only the mule knew that nothing was going to happen.

And you plan to leave it like that? the novelist asked.

Yes, of course! his neighbor replied. Any resolution

would inevitably spoil the suspense. But you're welcome to use the story—finish it if you like!

The novelist needed no further incentive. He hurried home and nine months later published part one of a hot new romance. The book became an instant bestseller and tantalized readers who eagerly awaited the sequel that never appeared.

The Return of
Little Red Riding Hood
in a Red Convertible

The girl goes driving in a red coupe sedan—no, make it a red convertible—to visit her dear old grandmother. This wolf tries to hitch a ride on the highway where you're not supposed to stop, and when he gets pushy she runs him right over. But the wolf, being resilient and conniving by nature, eats his way up through the body of the car (a cheap import) and into the heart of Little Red Riding Hood. Now the wolf is squirming inside and she can't get him out and there is no emergency medical service for miles— nor would they know what to do if there were one, never having delivered a young girl of an invasive wolf. But the beast won't let her be. You'll learn to live with me, he says. Like hell I will! says the headstrong girl, who always carries a nail file in her purse and cuts him out, endangered species be damned. And scornful of speed limits, she makes it to granny's with plenty of time to spare and whips up a tasty lunch of the leftovers. Granny gets indigestion and dies. Little Red inherits her pin cushion stuffed with precious

stones and her automatic rocking chair, drives off distraught at break-neck speed into the sunset and dies in a
car crash. The convertible is junked, later to be recycled in
the form of a thousand cans of Portuguese sardines pulled
off the shelves following a few reported fatal cases of
botulism.

Cityscape

Life twists like a snake through skyscraper forest and over the cement lawn. Only the barbed wire bush is still in bloom. At last we've conquered nature. I run past a mother wheeling a baby carriage. Don't see so many kids around anymore, I say to her in passing—not to speak of pregnant women, I mutter to myself. I bend forward to admire the baby. There I see a plump, rosy plastic doll lying in the carriage. The mother tugs on a skin-colored ring, a plastic belly button, which is attached to a thin, almost invisible thread. The doll rocks realistically back and forth and the pretty little thing starts crying. Then mother gives the ring another tug and the doll smiles sweetly, turns its cute, blond, curly head to me and whispers: My name is Lisa . . . Don't you love me? . . . I love *you*! So sweet! the proud mother declares. A beauty, I agree. And so practical! the young woman adds, Cries only when I'm in the mood. Don't you love me? . . . I love *you*! the artificial infant repeats again and again. That's enough, dear! mother scolds. And she pulls once again on the ring, whereupon the little darling yawns, obediently rolls over and falls fast asleep.

The Light of Your Looking Hurts My Eyes

Paint me up a man painting, annoyed at being watched. Turn your back, he cries, the light of your looking hurts my eyes. How well you express yourself for a painter, I flatter him, you should have been a poet. His head spins in an ecstasy of adulation, tracing a rapid self portrait in the air. When the spinning slows down some, the portrait turns into a Dutch landscape. Lovely, I say, lying. In fact, Dutch landscapes bore me to tears. Bravo, bravo, says the painter, slowing down even more, becoming a pure abstraction. Even his eyebrows signify nothing. I'll buy it, I say, proud of my contemporary taste.

The Fool
and
the Philosopher

A fool and a philosopher stood side by side in front of a mirror. I see an infinite number of possible worlds, the philosopher prognosticated, in which possible people motivated solely by pure logic and ideal ethical standards systematically enact all possible futures. Interesting, said the fool. And what do *you* see? the philosopher asked. The fool looked into every corner of the mirror. Then he scratched his head, shook his shoulders, raised his puzzled brow, turned his lower lip inside out and said: I see nothing but two fools.

The Nomad and the Wind

The wind. The wind begging me to take flight and I feel like a nomad locked in a prison cell who can no longer wander with his feet so that he must wander with his mind. When first locked away he would scratch a line on the stone wall for each new sun. By the time one whole wall was covered by these meaningless scratches he lost interest in the dreary procedure. The window was high above his head. He could see only a speck of the sky, and so he imagined the path of his tribe. Every footstep he imagined, from the camel's hooves to the barefoot shuffle of the children in the sand. He knew when they were tired and tasted their joy with them as they crouched in the shade of a palm tree chewing dates. The nomad talked with no one. He did not even nod to the jailer who left a pail of food for him each morning and came by to pick up the empty again at night. The nomad thought of the wind, of the footsteps that his people made in the sand, and how quickly these footsteps disappeared. When the jailer began to find the food pail untouched he was only too happy to sell the extra portion to another prisoner. At first it made the nomad sad to think of the vanishing footsteps of his people. Each imprint in the sand was precious to him. Then he thought of the ever-changing pattern of the sand and he smiled: How wise is the wind, my people wander and no man can follow them. The jailer swore he had never seen such a peaceful smile on the face of a dead man.

The Intruder

Last night an indigent long-haired intruder camped out in our family garden and laughed when I demanded that he leave. And the longer he stayed the fatter he grew. Bit by bit, he began to eat up our house and to defecate out what he could not digest as rubble. In a fit of rage and frustration I picked up lumps of his undigested domesticity (now petrified) and flung it at him. No, no! You can't do that! It isn't nice to strike your father, my mother protested. But the more rubble I flung at him, the more he shrank, until with one last toss I reduced him to a flatulent eruption that disappeared in a gust of wind.

Mother of God

In a pan of lukewarm water I find a gray aborted fetus. It speaks to me with sensitivity and intelligence. I love it and adopt it as my child. We have many fine talks and walks together. Then the real mother returns and finds the tiny body intact but the head is missing and water bubbles up through the loose umbilical cord. The mother seems less upset than annoyed. No doubt she had heard of the famous fetus and merely wanted to claim her rights as the Mother of God.

How the Face Ages

The cheeks collapse around the nose. The eyes sink back into their sockets. Memory furrows the brow, amnesia sinks into the jowls. The mouth and eyes sprout subsidiaries, the way great rivers do. The shrubbery above the eyes and mouth grows wild, an untended hedge and a scraggly lawn. The symmetry, so painstakingly cultivated once, dissolves into a willful dissonance. Eyes, identical no longer, now slouch side by side: two brothers different in age and temperament who may not even share the same father. The lips droop, weary of a life of enforced smiling. The forehead swells and the cheekbones protrude, giving a false air of wisdom and sensitivity. In fact, it is only the skull reasserting itself. The skin, formerly so pink, elastic and hopeful, now sags like one of those native rope suspension bridges that hold just long enough for the hero to make his escape but disintegrate as soon as the enemy attempts the crossing. At this late stage, smiles and frowns are equally risky, either may sink the skin forever into the abyss of bone.

219

I Stand Possessionless
at the Gate
of the Living

A Catholic-like cult religion has cars that for a small donation will drive the living back to visit the dead. I run, having just missed the preliminary rites, tear open the trunk, push out the divider between boot and back seat and leap in. But the space is too narrow, I cannot squeeze through, and as the car starts rolling, I am caught with my head among the faithful and my feet dangling free. I give up the journey, but meanwhile, an altarboy who claims he meant well says he flung my belongings in after me. And now, as the car drives off to the dead, I stand possession-less at the gate of the living.

An Afterword

Death resumes where birth left off, but the living must still plod along, invent a destiny.

And prior to the final defecation, when the old man's face grows boyish once again with wonder, those looking on must reassure themselves that the entity about to expire did have a shoe size and fingernails that needed to be clipped.